Next Stop, a Hanging

After they were detrained at Paso del Muerte, Win and Joe led their horses to the tree where they'd spotted a man hanging. Whoever hanged him had not put a hood over his face, leaving the grotesque visage of a violent death for all to see. The worst part about him was his eyes. They were bulging nearly out of their sockets. Win pulled a sign off the corpse's boot.

" 'Luke Grant,' " Win read. " 'Leave him be. He'll hang here as a warning against all other cattle rustlers.' And it's signed by a fella named Claymore."

Joe mounted his horse, then rode up close enough to be able to reach the rope. Taking out his pocketknife, he cut the rope, and the body fell. "Well," he said, "whether Claymore likes cattle rustlers or not, I already don't like the son of a bitch."

DON'T MISS THESE
ALL-ACTION WESTERN SERIES
FROM THE BERKLEY PUBLISHING GROUP

THE GUNSMITH by J. R. Roberts
Clint Adams was a legend among lawmen, outlaws, and ladies.
They called him . . . the Gunsmith.

LONGARM by Tabor Evans
The popular long-running series about U.S. Deputy Marshal
Long—his life, his loves, his fight for justice.

SLOCUM by Jake Logan
Today's longest-running action Western. John Slocum rides
a deadly trail of hot blood and cold steel.

BUSHWHACKERS by B. J. Lanagan
An action-packed series by the creators of Longarm! The
rousing adventures of the most brutal gang of cutthroats ever
assembled—Quantrill's Raiders.

BUSHWHACKERS

DEATH PASS

B. J. Lanagan

JOVE BOOKS, NEW YORK

DEATH PASS

A Jove Book / published by arrangement with
the author

PRINTING HISTORY
Jove edition / October 1999

All rights reserved.
Copyright © 1999 by Penguin Putnam Inc.
This book may not be reproduced in whole or in part,
by mimeograph or any other means, without permission.
For information address: The Berkley Publishing Group,
a division of Penguin Putnam Inc.,
375 Hudson Street, New York, New York 10014.

The Penguin Putnam Inc. World Wide Web site address is
http://www.penguinputnam.com

ISBN: 0-515-12658-6

A JOVE BOOK®
Jove Books are published by The Berkley Publishing Group,
a division of Penguin Putnam Inc.,
375 Hudson Street, New York, New York 10014.
JOVE and the "J" design
are trademarks belonging to Penguin Putnam Inc.

PRINTED IN THE UNITED STATES OF AMERICA

10 9 8 7 6 5 4 3 2 1

BUSHWHACKERS

DEATH PASS

Chapter 1

SOMEWHERE IN THE PRE-DAWN DARKNESS A CALF BAWLED anxiously and its mother answered. In the distance a coyote sent up its long, lonesome wail, while out in the pond, frogs thrummed their night song. The moon was a thin sliver of silver, but the night was alive with stars ... from the very bright, shining lights all the way down to those stars that weren't visible as individual bodies at all, but whose glow added to the luminous powder that dusted the distant sky.

Around the milling shapes of shadows that made up the small herd rode three cowboys. One was much younger than the other two. Known as "nighthawks," their job was to keep watch over the herd during the night, then turn them over to the drovers in the morning for the short drive into the railhead at Paso del Muerte.

The night had been long, and in order to stay awake the three young men were engaged in conversation.

"What do you mean? Are you trying to tell me you've never even *had* a woman?" one of the older cowboys asked the youngest one.

The youngest cowboy, whose name was Billy, cleared his throat in embarrassment. "I'm only sixteen. I guess I ain't never give it that much thought."

"Why, boy, don't you know you can never be a man until you go upstairs at Big Kate's Place?"

"With Big Kate," the other added.

"With . . . with Big Kate?" Billy asked in a plaintive voice that was decidedly void of any enthusiasm over the prospect.

"Hell yes, with Big Kate. Big Kate owns the place. That means ever'body who comes in there has to go with her first."

"Tell you what," the first cowboy said. "Why don't we ride into Paso del Muerte first thing after we get off work? It'll be daytime, there won't hardly be nobody else there, an' we can have our pick."

"All except Billy," the second cowboy insisted. "He has to go upstairs with Big Kate."

"Well, yeah, but then he can go upstairs with anyone he wants to."

" 'Cept whoever me an' you has already took for our ownselves."

The calf's call for his mother came again, this time with more insistence. The mother's answer had a degree of anxiousness to it.

"Sounds like one of 'em's wandered off," Billy said. "Maybe I'd better go find it."

"Hell, why bother? It'll find its own way back."

"I don't mind," Billy said, slapping his legs against the sides of his horse and riding off, disappearing in the darkness.

One of the cowboys laughed a low, knowing laugh. "If you ask me, Billy's just anxious to get away from us before we talk him into actually going upstairs with Big Kate."

"Who knows?" the other teased. "Maybe we can convince him she's just what he needs."

"I'd hate to see the fella that really needs her." Both cowboys laughed at their joke.

Suddenly, from the darkness came a loud, blood-curdling scream filled with such terror that both cowboys shivered all the way down to their boots.

"What the hell was that?"

They heard the sound of galloping hooves, then, from the darkness, Billy's horse, its nostrils flared wide and its eyes wild with terror, came running by them, its saddle empty.

"My God, where's Billy?"

"That was Billy that screamed!"

Though both were wearing guns, neither man was actually

a gunman. Nevertheless, their friend was in trouble, and feeling the unfamiliar weight of pistols in their hand, they rode into the darkness, to his aid.

A moment later, gunshots erupted in the night, the muzzle-flashes lighting up the herd.

"Jesus! What's happening? Who is it? They're all around us!" one of the cowboys shouted in terror, firing his gun wildly in the dark.

The two young men tried to fight back but they were young, inexperienced, scared, and outnumbered. In less than a minute, both had been shot from their saddles and then the night grew still, save for the restless shuffle of the herd of cattle.

At some distance away from all this, a short but powerfully-built man sat on his horse with his hat pulled low over a bald head and browless eyes. Though he had put everything in motion, he had not personally taken part in the proceedings. Now one of the other men, with the smell of death still in his nostrils, rode up to him.

"That's it, Potter," the rider said. "We kilt all three of them cowboys and took a look all around the herd. There ain't no one else ridin' nighthawk."

"Good. Now take the cows," Potter ordered in a hoarse whisper.

Six weeks later, and forty miles south of Paso del Muerte, Win and Joe Coulter stopped to give their horses a few minutes' rest. Joe took a long pull from his canteen, wiped the back of his hand across his mouth, recorked the canteen and hooked it over the pommel of his saddle.

"Say, Win, you remember how Mom used to fry pork chops, breaded in milk and biscuit crumbs? Then she'd serve 'em up with a side of turnip greens, swimming in bacon grease and doused with hot pepper sauce, and a mess of fried potatoes, with eggs scrambled in 'em. You remember that?"

Win chuckled. "Why, Joe, I'm hurt. The way you're talking makes me think you don't care much for what we've been eating lately."

"Eating?" Joe scoffed. "Are you calling what we've been

doing eating? Far as I'm concerned, beans and jerky ain't eating.''

''Then what is it?''

''It's just staying alive, that's all,'' Joe said. He climbed back onto his horse. ''Staying alive,'' he repeated.

''You're just tired,'' Win suggested. ''You'll feel better once we get into a town, sleep in a bed, and eat something that wasn't cooked over a trail fire.''

''You got that right, Big Brother. I am tired, all right,'' Joe said.

Win and Joe had a right to be tired. They had been on the trail for the better part of three weeks. It had been a long, hard ride, and both brothers were butt-sore and saddle-weary. But the tiredness went much deeper than mere trail weariness. It was a tiredness from which they would never get relief, for they were committed to a lifetime of living on the edge. Win and Joe Coulter, known in some circles as the Bushwhackers, belonged to that restless band of souls who were unable to pick up the peaceful lives they had known before the war.

They had ridden for the Missouri border ruffian, William C. Quantrill. Though Quantrill's irregulars were never fully accepted as an official part of the Confederate army, riding with his bunch had served Win and Joe well. That was because the Coulter brothers were motivated not so much by patriotism toward the Confederacy but by a blood-lust revenge against the Kansas Jayhawkers who had slaughtered their parents and burned their farm.

The boys got their revenge, but it had come at a high price. When the war was over the regular soldiers of blue and gray returned home. Not so the men who had ridden with Quantrill and Bloody Bill Anderson. They returned not as war heros, but as wanted men.

Win and Joe Coulter got out of Missouri just ahead of a hangman's rope. They were now nomads, wandering through the West as rootless as tumbleweeds. They eyed every stranger suspiciously and entered each town with muscles tense, ready, if need be, for a lightning-fast draw and a deadly accurate shot.

Now, late in the afternoon of their twenty-first day on the

trail, they approached the little town of Sulphur Springs. It rose from the hot, sun-baked earth like a series of low lumps of clay and rock. Sulphur Springs was a one-street town that had grown up at this location to take advantage of the only water in the area, even though, as the name attested, that water was of questionable quality.

They surveyed the town as they rode in. Since the war there had been hundreds of towns like this, and there was almost an ethereal quality to them. Sulphur Springs was like all the other towns, faced by houses of rip-sawed lumber, false-fronted businesses, and a few sod buildings.

It had rained earlier in the day, and the street was a quagmire. The mud, worked into the consistency of quicksand by horses' hooves, had mixed with the droppings to become one long, stinking, sucking pool of ooze. When the rain stopped the sun, yellow and hot in its late afternoon transit, had begun the process of evaporation. The result was a foul miasma rising from the street.

The saloon wasn't hard to find. It was the biggest and grandest building in the entire town. Shadows gave the illusion of coolness inside the saloon, but it was only an illusion. The dozen and a half customers who were drinking had to keep their bandannas handy to wipe the sweat from their faces.

Anytime Win and Joe entered a strange saloon they were on the alert, and this one was no different. As they surveyed the place, they did so with such calm that the average person would think it no more than a glance of idle curiosity. In reality, it was a very thorough appraisal of the room. They were checking out who was armed, what type of weapons they were carrying, and whether or not those who were armed were wearing their guns in such a way as to indicate that they knew how to use them.

They also checked to see if there was anyone they knew, or more specifically, if there was anyone who reacted as if they might know them. It was particularly important for them to pick out such people, for their reputations were such that there were many more people who knew them than they knew. And because their lives since the war had been as violent as during the war, there was nearly always someone gunning for them for one reason or another.

None of the drinkers seemed to pose a problem. From all they could tell, there were only cowboys and drifters here, and less than half of them were even wearing guns. A couple of the cowboys were wearing their guns low and kicked-out, gunfighter style, but Win and Joe could tell at a glance that it was all for show. They were certain they had never used them for anything but target practice, and probably were not very successful at that.

The bartender stood at the end of the bar, wiping the used glasses with his stained apron, then setting them among the unused glasses. When he saw Win and Joe step up to the bar, he moved down toward them.

"What'll it be, gents?"

"Two beers," Win said. The bartender started to turn away.

"And I'll have the same," Joe added.

Smiling, the bartender nodded, then went to work filling the glasses from the barrel.

"I didn't see a hotel as I rode in," Win said.

"That's 'cause we ain't got one," the bartender answered. He cut his eyes upward. "Got some rooms upstairs though."

"How much?"

"Depends whether you want 'em for sleepin', or for sportin'."

"For sleeping."

"Three dollars."

"Three dollars?" Joe said. "That's a little high, isn't it? How much if we took them for sporting?"

"Three dollars," the bartender replied.

"That's the same thing."

"Yep. Thing is, if you're sleepin' in 'em, they can't be used for sportin', and the girls will be losin' money."

"What do you say, Joe?" Win asked.

Joe sighed. "I don't plan to sleep on the ground tonight. I say we take it."

Chapter 2

WIN FINISHED HIS SECOND BEER.

"We'll have another," Joe said to the bartender.

"No, wait, not me," Win said.

Joe looked at him in surprise. "I never knew you to turn down a beer," he said.

"The beer will be here when I come back down," Win said. "In the meantime, I'm going to take a bath. I've got several days of trail stink on me."

"Yeah, I been meanin' to say something about that, Big Brother," Joe teased, making a face and waving his hand in front of his nose. "Why do you think I've been staying upwind from you?"

Win laughed. "You're one to talk. You could put a skunk to shame."

"That may be," Joe said, taking the fresh beer the bartender had put before him. "But I can live with my own smell. At least, 'till I have me a few more beers and get a little somethin' to eat."

Win laughed at his brother, then climbed the stairs to the room he had been told would be his for the night. From the red textured wallpaper and the pink flounced curtains, Win could see that this wasn't an ordinary room. There was also a wooden bathtub, and almost as soon as he had the door open, a hotel employee appeared with a bucket of hot water.

Ten minutes later little wisps of steam were rising from the tub as Win slipped down into it. Fifteen minutes later, with his skin red from the hot water and soapy scrub, he dried off and walked over to lay on the bed. Still naked from his bath, he crawled between the stiff, clean sheets. He was asleep in moments.

When he opened his eyes, much later, the room was dark. Something had awakened him, but as yet he didn't know what it was.

Then he heard a soft rattle of the doorknob. He was on his feet instantly, and like a stalking cat, moved to the side of the door. He cocked his pistol and held it at the ready. Still nude, he could feel an evening breeze pushing through the window, and the texture of the boards under feet. He was intensely alert, ready for anything.

Someone was breathing on the other side of the door. The hall lanterns were lit, and a sliver of light shot in under the door. From the saloon below, he could hear the nighttime revelry, a playing piano, and someone laughing.

Win waited.

The doorknob turned again and the door began to swing open, spilling an ever-widening wedge of light into the room.

Win watched the back of the door ease toward him.

A shadow filled the light, gliding in through the opening, backlit by the lantern on the wall in the hall beyond.

"What the hell?" Win whispered in surprise, letting his breath escape in a rush. The person trying to get into his room was a woman.

Win grabbed the woman's arm and pulled her inside. He closed the door quickly behind her, the motion pulling her against him. She let out a cry of alarm.

"Who are you?" Win asked, backing away from her.

"My name is Irene Goodwin," the woman replied in a frightened voice.

"What are you doing here, Irene?" Win asked. He lowered his pistol, but didn't put it away.

"I live here," Irene said. "This is my room."

Win stood quietly for a moment. He knew he had rented a sporting room, but he hadn't really considered the fact that he might be sharing it.

"Oh," Win said, sheepishly.

"I'm sorry if I startled you," Irene said. She smiled. "But I really didn't expect to find you like this." She looked pointedly at Win's nudity.

Win shrugged, then backed into the shadows and wrapped himself in a bed sheet.

"You're lucky I'm not the kind that shoots first," Win said. "You could've gotten yourself killed, real easy. Did you know that?"

Irene shook her head. "I'm sorry," she said. "I guess I just didn't think. I wanted to see you. . . ." she paused in midsentence, then laughed, a small, throaty laugh. "I just didn't plan to see so much of you," she added.

Win chuckled. "I guess you did see more than you bargained for," he said. "Why did you want to see me?"

"Downstairs they are saying that you and the other one, the big man who came with you, are called the Bushwhackers. You're supposed to be very good with guns. Is that true?"

Win nodded. "We have some experience with them."

"I would like to hire you. Both of you."

"Hire us? Hire us for what?"

"To find the man who killed my brother," Irene said.

"Do you have any idea who did it?"

Irene shook her head. "Cattle rustlers, but I don't know who they were. All I know is that Billy, and the two cowboys with him, were murdered, and the cows they were watching were stolen."

"I wish I could help you, Irene. But what you need is a lawman, and I'm not in the lawman business."

Irene sighed. "I was sort of hoping that since you and Mr. Truelove knew each other during the war, you might be willing to help him, if not me."

"Truelove? Otis Truelove?"

Irene nodded her head.

"What does he have to do with it?"

"He owns the ranch where my brother and the other two cowboys worked," Irene said. "When I went to the funeral, I asked Mr. Truelove if he had any idea who killed Billy. He said he knew who it was. He said everyone knew who it was.

It was an outlaw named Emil Potter. Potter has been harassing all the ranchers in the valley.''

''If they know who it is, why doesn't the law arrest him?''

''I asked Mr. Truelove that. He said it was more than the marshal could handle. He said it would take someone like you and your brother.''

''I don't know why he would say that,'' Win said. ''We aren't lawmen, and we certainly aren't vigilantes.''

''He didn't say you were. It was my idea to try and hire you. Especially after all the things he said about you.''

''What did he say about my brother and me?''

''He said that he had met you during the war, and he considered you to be honorable men. I was hoping that maybe, because you were friends, you would . . .''

''We were not friends,'' Win said, interrupting her.

Irene looked confused. ''You mean you didn't know him?''

''We knew him, all right. We just weren't friends.''

''I don't understand.''

''Easy enough to understand,'' Win said. ''Otis Truelove fought for the North, my brother and I fought for the South. We were enemies.''

''Enemies? And yet, he thinks so highly of you,'' Irene said. ''How odd.''

''It isn't all that odd if you understand war,'' Win said. He paused for a moment. ''My brother and I were planning to go through Paso del Muerte anyway. Maybe we'll stop by and visit Truelove.''

''Oh, thank you!'' Irene said.

Win shook his head and held up his hand. ''I'm not agreeing to anything,'' he said. ''I just said I'll stop by and have a visit with Truelove.''

''That's enough for me,'' Irene said. ''If you are honorable men, as Mr. Truelove says, then I know you will do the right thing.'' She stood there for a long moment, looking at Win. Then she laughed.

''What is it?''

''Wrapped up in that bed sheet the way you are, you look like one of those Roman senators.''

Win looked down at himself. "Yeah, I guess I do at that," he said, chuckling.

Irene walked over to him and reached up for the corner of the sheet. He did nothing to stop her, and a moment later he was nude again. She began removing her own clothes.

"Are you still trying to persuade me?" Win asked.

Irene shook her head. "Not exactly. You've got this one coming, remember? You've already paid for it."

As soon as she was naked, she leaned into him, then kissed him. Win's tongue darted into the wet, soft cavern of her mouth. Her hands moved over his arms and shoulders, where they squeezed and massaged. Her fingers teased along his chest.

They moved to the bed where Win grazed lower with his kisses, along her jawline, then to her ear. He inserted his tongue into her ear and made her gasp and stiffen. Then he trailed his tongue down the long column of her throat to her shoulder, and down across the soft, smooth flesh of her breast to touch his tongue to the nipple. He took it between his teeth, gently, then began to suck.

"Oh, yes," Irene murmured. "Oh, this feels so good."

Irene kissed his forehead, while her body thrashed beneath him. Then, once she was under him, she spread her legs in invitation. Grabbing him, she guided him into her. She was moist, slippery-ready, and begging.

Win withheld his thrust for just an instant to kiss her again. He pushed his tongue into her silken mouth and his manhood into her velvet cleft at the same time. She thrust her hips up as hard as she could, as he buried himself into her long, hot, pulsing tunnel.

Irene bucked wildly, gyrating her hips, forcing him to go deep and fast, squeezing him with intense little muscle spasms.

Win rode her hard, thrust deep, withdrew, thrust in again. Beneath him, Irene cried out brokenly and crashed over the peak of her first orgasm, then moved quickly in quest of another. She muttered, moaned, and tried to take him deeper. Lightning struck her again, and she shuddered with the pleasure of it.

Every stroke was faster and deeper. The lightning returned

and Irene, writhing with pleasure, spread the fire from her body to Win's. Win felt the sweet-hot boiling of his own juices as he exploded into her, sliding through her hot-oil slippery tunnel to deposit his seed.

Afterward, they lay side by side for several moments without touching and without talking. Outside, the evening commerce of Sulphur Springs continued, unaffected by what happened in here. Two men walked by on the sidewalk below, their boots making loud clumps on the board planks, their voices raised in conversation, intense only to them. In the bar below, the out-of-tune piano continued its tinkling. There was a woman's shrill scream, not of fear but of frolic, followed by a burst of laughter. At the far end of town a dog barked, and out on the prairie a coyote called for its mate.

For a moment it was nice. Win could almost believe that he belonged there.

Suddenly, Irene broke the mood when she sat up in bed. "Well, I can't lie here all night," she said. "I've got work to do."

"What the hell? You won't be bringing anyone in here?" Win asked.

Irene laughed at the idea. "Now, that would make a pretty picture, wouldn't it? Me and a gentleman in bed and you sitting over on the chair waiting until we were finished." She laughed again.

"I don't think it's a damn bit funny," Win said.

Irene smiled down at him as she got dressed.

"Don't worry, hon," she said. "We have rooms at the far end of the hall for the short dates. This room is only for overnighters . . . which you are." Fully dressed now, she leaned over and kissed him on the forehead. "I'll see you again at eleven."

"You're coming back?"

"Yes, of course. I sleep here, remember? That is, if you let me sleep," she added in a husky voice.

"You can sleep in the daytime," Win said.

Irene paused in the door and looked back toward the bed, and the man she had just been with. "I could at that," she said.

• • •

Downstairs, Joe, fed and with his thirst satisfied, had forgotten all about bed. He was playing poker, and it was one of those nights when everything was going right. He could almost will the cards he needed into his hand. Holding a pair of jacks, he had just called for three more cards. When he picked up two more jacks, it was all he could do to keep the smile off his face. It was his bet.

"Five dollars," he said.

"Mister, I think you're bluffing," one of the other players said with an expression of confidence on his face. "I'm going to raise that to twenty-five dollars."

Now, Joe made no attempt whatever to keep the smile off his face.

"Let's bump it up to a hundred," he said, sliding the money to the center of the table.

The player who had called his bluff knew he had stepped into it, and the expression of confidence was replaced by one of chagrin. He started to call Joe, but thought better of it.

"It's your pot," he said.

Chapter 3

PASO DEL MUERTE WAS A GOOD FORTY MILES WEST, AND though the boys could have ridden their horses, Joe's poker winnings enabled them to take the train. They arranged to have their horses shipped in the stock car, while they took a seat in the day coach. It was an easy way to travel and they sat looking out the window of the train as the terrain rolled by.

True to her promise, Irene had returned at eleven the night before. But finding Win asleep, and being tired herself, she had merely slipped into bed beside him. When Win woke up that morning, he'd left without waking her.

He did think about what she had told him though. It had been interesting to learn about what had happened to Lieutenant Otis Truelove since the war's end. Win leaned back in his seat, propped his knees up on the seat-back before him, tipped his hat down over his eyes, and drifted off to another time, remembering a battle that was fought long ago, and far away.

Because of the ebb and flow of the battle, the dead and wounded were scattered over a wide area. The fighting had left many casualties on both sides, and during the night their moans and cries could be heard even above the thunderous drumming of the rain and the incessant boom of artillery. The sound was heart-rending, even to the most hardened ears.

Most of the wounded were calling for water, so Win and Joe collected half a dozen canteens and started out onto the battlefield. Fortunately, the rain stopped shortly after they went out, but the night was still dark and overcast, without moon or stars to light the way.

Win and Joe weren't the only ones who went out, and because the night was so dark, many of the men who prowled the battleground were carrying lanterns to help them distinguish the wounded from the dead. As a result, the battlefield looked like a great meadow filled with giant fireflies, with the lanterns bobbing about from point to point.

A breeze came up, carrying on its breath a damp chill. Win pulled his coat about him and continued on his mission of mercy, picking his way across roads and fields, now littered with the residue of battle: weapons, equipment, and among the discards, the dead and dying.

"Water," a weak voice called, and Win halted. "I beg of you, sir, be you Union or Reb, if you are a God-fearing man, you'll give me water."

"Yes," Win said. "I have water." Moving quickly to the soldier, he saw that it was a Yankee officer, an infantry lieutenant. He uncorked the canteen and knelt down by the officer, then lifted his head.

"Here you go, Yank," he said.

"Bless you," the wounded soldier replied.

Win heard the metallic click of a pistol being cocked.

"Don't go wasting water on that Yank. I'm about to kill him," a cold voice said.

Win looked toward the man who had spoken and saw a Confederate officer. The officer was quite small for a full-grown man. He was just over five-feet-two inches tall, and couldn't have weighed more than 125 pounds. He had blotchy red skin, watery blue eyes, and a large, beak-like nose. Win didn't recognize him, but that was understandable, as there had been thousands of men from both sides committed to this fight. There was no way Win could know everyone.

"I'm not going to deny this man a drink of water just because he is wearing a blue uniform," Win said.

"Don't think that because you're wearing gray I won't shoot you," the Confederate officer replied. "As far as I'm concerned, he and all the rest of the Yankee trash out here* *can die of thirst, and I'll shoot anyone who tries to help them.''*

"If you are going to shoot, go ahead and shoot," Win said resolutely. "But this man's going to have water on his lips when we die." Once again, he turned the canteen up to the Yankee officer's lips, and the wounded man began drinking thirstily.

"You son of a bitch! I warned you!" the Confederate officer shouted. That was as far as he got. An instant before he could pull the trigger, there was a rather solid-sounding thump as Joe, who had come up behind him, hit him over the head.

"Did you kill him?" Win asked. There was a nonchalance to his voice that belied the situation.

"No," Joe said, kneeling down beside the man he had just hit. "He's still alive, but he's going to have one hell of a headache when he wakes up."

"Thank you," the wounded Yankee said, as he took his fill of water. "You are a true gentleman." Seeing Joe come over to join them, the young officer added. "Both of you."

"Where are you hit?" Win asked.

"In the leg."

Win held the lantern down toward the wound as he and Joe examined it. "What do you think, Joe?"

"The bleeding has pretty much stopped. I think if he can get back to his surgeon and have the bullet taken out before it festers, he'll be all right," Joe said.

"You think you can walk?" Win asked.

"I don't know. I'll try."

"We'll help."

With Win on one side and Joe on the other, they got the young officer on his feet, then began walking him toward the Union lines.

"My name is Truelove," the young officer said. "Lieutenant Otis Truelove. Who might you gentlemen be?"

"I'm Win Coulter. This is my brother, Joe," Win said.

"You're with General Sterling Price?"

"In a manner of speaking. Our group just joined with him for this battle. We're with Quantrill."

Truelove gasped. "Quantrill?" After a moment's silence he

continued. "*Maybe you should leave me here,*" he suggested. "*I can make it the rest of the way on my own.*"

"*We'll take you a little closer,*" Joe said. "*What's the matter. Does it bother you because we are with Quantrill?*"

"*Yes,*" Truelove admitted. "*But I'm worried for you, not for me. You may not know this, but the orders are out. If any of Quantrill's men are captured . . .*"

"*We are not to be treated as prisoners of war, but as criminals,*" Win said. "*Yes, we've seen the orders.*"

"*But, don't you understand? If you are captured tonight, you'll be dead by sun up. They'll hang you.*"

"*They haven't caught us yet,*" Joe said.

"*Shh,*" Win whispered. "*We're nearly to the Yankee lines. No sense in announcing our presence.*"

Win's warning was too late. From the darkness in front of them, two Yankee soldiers suddenly appeared. Both were carrying rifles, and they had the rifles in the ready position.

"*Halt!*" one of them called. "*Who's there?*"

"*Yankee pickets,*" Joe said under his breath.

"*Soldiers, I am Liutenant Otis Truelove, of the Seventh Kansas,*" Truelove said.

The soldiers looked at Truelove. His blue uniform clearly announced who he was. Win and Joe were wearing gray.

"*Who are these men? They look like Confederates,*" one of the pickets challenged.

"*They are from General Price's staff,*" Truelove said quickly. "*They have been guaranteed safe passage to bring me back to my own lines.*"

"*I don't see no flag of truce or anything,*" one of the Yankee pickets said.

"*They can scarcely show the flag while carrying me, can they?*" Truelove challenged.

"*No, sir, I don't reckon they can,*" the picket replied.

Truelove looked at Win and Joe. "*Thank you very much for your help,*" Truelove said. "*But I expect you two had better get back to General Price now, before your safe passage expires.*"

"*I reckon so,*" Win said. "*Good luck to you.*"

When Truelove saw that one of the pickets was looking sus-

piciously at Win and Joe, he put his hand on the picket's shoulder.

"This is no place to stand around gabbing," Truelove said. "Why don't you two men help me back to the aid station? I have a mine ball in my leg, and it's going to have to come out."

"Yes, sir," the picket said.

With their attention diverted, Win and Joe were able to go back across no man's land.

"I'm sure glad that Yankee lied for us," Joe said. He put his finger in his collar, then pulled it away from his neck. "I wouldn't have taken too highly to hanging in the morning."

"Yes, but if anyone saw you hit a Confederate officer, our own people may hang us," Win said.

"You're right. I'm sorry I hit him."

Win looked at Joe in surprise? "You're sorry you hit him?"

"Yeah. I should've killed the son of a bitch."

"Paso del Muerte! We're comin' into Paso del Muerte, folks," the conductor called, walking quickly through the car. Win wasn't sure if he had been napping or just remembering, but at the conductor's call, he pushed his hat back and looked out the window as the train began creaking to a stop in the depot. Something outside the window caught his attention, and he sat up for a closer look.

"What the hell?" he said. "Joe?"

"Yeah, I see it," Joe replied, staring through the window at the same thing that had caught Win's eye.

A large cottonwood tree stood in an empty lot just east of the railroad depot. There, hanging from one of the high, straight limbs of the Cottonwood, was a corpse. The corpse's hands were tied behind its back and the head and neck were misshapen by the effect of the hanging. The corpse was twisting slowly at the end of the rope.

"Looks like there's a sign or something tacked onto his boot," Win said.

The two brothers got off, then walked up to the stock car to get their horses. The horses were a little skittish from the journey and had to be coaxed down the ramp.

When the horses were detrained, Win glanced again at the body that was hanging from the tree.

"Joe, you see anything odd about that?" Win asked, nodding toward the body.

"Odd?" Joe replied. "Hell no, what's odd about seeing a corpse hanging from a tree, right in the middle of town?" he teased.

"Yeah, well, that," Win said. "But the other thing is, there is nobody standing around looking at it. You'd think someone would be curious, wouldn't you?"

"You would think," Joe agreed.

"I am."

Joe chuckled. "I thought you might be."

"Let's go see what the sign says."

The two men led their horses into the empty lot, then stood under the tree and looked up at the man who was hanging there. Whoever hanged him had not put a hood over his face, thus leaving the grotesque visage of a violent death for all to see. The skin was chalky white, the cheeks were puffed, and the mouth was open. Flies were crawling in and out of the mouth. The worst part about him was his eyes. They were bulging nearly out of their sockets.

"Ever see him before?" Joe asked.

"No," Win said. "The way this fella is all puffed up though, I'm not sure I would recognize him even if I had seen him." Win pulled the sign off the corpse's boot.

"What does it say?" Joe asked.

" 'Luke Grant,' " Win read. " 'Leave him be. He'll hang here as a warning against all other cattle rustlers.' And it's signed by a fella named Claymore. Hmm, sounds like this fella Claymore doesn't much care for cattle rustlers," Win concluded.

"Well, whether Claymore likes cattle rustlers or not, I already don't like the son of a bitch," Joe said. He mounted his horse, then rode up close enough to be able to reach the rope. Taking out his pocket-knife, he cut the rope, and the body fell.

"What are you going to do with him?" Win asked.

"I don't know. Take him to the undertaker, I guess. There has to be one in town," Joe answered.

Looking around, Win saw a baggage cart by the edge of the depot. He brought the cart over, then he and Joe loaded the body onto it. Tossing a rope around the cart, the two brothers started riding toward town, pulling the cart with the body behind them.

Although there hadn't been anyone standing in the empty lot while the body was hanging, word quickly passed through the town that the body had been cut down, and as the two brothers pulled the cart down the street, a small crowd began to follow them. Most of the onlookers stayed to the side of the street, looking on in curiosity, but three men suddenly stepped out into the street in front of them. One of them was young, dressed in black. He had a silver band around his hat and his gunbelt was studded with silver conchos. Even his pistol was silver-plated and pearl-handled. He had an arrogant sneer on his face. The other two men hung back a step, deferring to the young, arrogant one.

"Get down off them horses," the arrogant one ordered.

Win and Joe looked at each other, then with a shrug, dismounted and stepped up to the men.

"What are you doin' with that?" the man in black asked.

Joe and Win looked toward the body, then back at the three men who challenged them.

"We found him," Joe replied.

"I know where you found 'im. What are you doing with him?"

"Well, I thought maybe we would take him to the undertaker's," Joe answered easily. "Maybe you can tell us where it is."

"Mister, maybe you didn't see the sign we left tacked to the son of a bitch's foot," the arrogant one said.

"Oh, you mean the one that said, 'Leave him be?' Yes, we saw it," Win said.

"Then you know we figured to leave this cattle thief hanging for a while."

"That's not a good idea," Win replied as if discussing possibilities with them. "He's already beginning to get a little ripe. Besides which, it doesn't make a very good impression on anyone who might be coming in on the train, to see a corpse hanging there like that.''

"That ain't none of your concern. Now, take 'im back, and hang up where you found him.''

"I can't,'' Win said. "He won't let me.''

The leader of the group looked confused. "He won't let you? *Who* won't let you?''

"My little brother won't let me,'' Win said, nodding toward Joe. "He's got his heart set on seeing this fella get a proper burying. And as you can see, he's a pretty good-sized man. When he sets his heart on something, he pretty much gets his way.''

As if unable to believe what he was hearing, the arrogant one looked at the two men with him.

"Did you hear what he said?''

"Yeah, Harley, we heard 'im,'' one of the two men said.

Harley stretched his face into what one might suppose was a smile, though it came out as little more than a grotesque sneer. "Looks like we're going to have three bodies hanging from the tree,'' he said. "The one we done hung, and these two we're about to shoot.''

"Wait a minute. There's three of you and only two of us. This isn't fair,'' Win complained.

Harley laughed. "Well, now, mister, life is like that sometimes.''

"Yeah, I know,'' Win said, sighing. "It looks like I'm only going to get one of you. Joe will get the other two.''

"What?''

"Which one do you want, Big Brother?'' Joe asked, calmly.

"Well, since I'm only going to get one, I think I'd like to take this loudmouthed little son of a bitch they're callin' Harley,'' Win replied.

Harely turned to the others. "Will you listen to this? You'd think he . . . oof!''

That was as far as he got, because Win suddenly, and unexpectedly sent a vicious kick right between the man's legs, scoring a direct hit with the point of his boot. Grunting in surprise and pain, Harley doubled over, then went down. Win's sudden move had caught the others by such surprise that they looked at their fallen partner in shock.

Joe caught one of the remaining two men with a powerful roundhouse right to the chin. He went down and out like a light, alongside Harley, who was now lying in the dirt, moaning in pain.

By the time the third man realized he was the only one left, it was too late. Joe dropped him with a well-aimed punch as well.

The townspeople who had been following the boys from the moment Joe had cut the body down now cheered and crowded out into the street around them.

"Any of you know where we might find the undertaker?" Joe asked.

Two of the men pointed to a little building down the street, but neither of them spoke.

"Thanks," Joe said.

Chapter 4

REMOUNTING, WIN AND JOE CONTINUED THEIR RIDE DOWN the middle of the street of Paso del Muerte, passing in and out of the splashes of light that spilled from the adjacent buildings. Behind them, the steel-banded wheels of the little baggage cart they were pulling rang as they rolled across the hard-packed dirt. Farther behind still, the three men who had accosted them were just beginning to regain consciousness. Much of the town continued to follow, though they kept to either side of the street, maintaining what they figured would be a safe distance from Win and Joe.

Leaving the body with an undertaker who was somewhat less than enthusiastic over getting the business, the brothers' next stop was the nearest saloon. Again, they were followed by a score or more townspeople.

Joe laughed.

"What is it?" Win asked.

"So much for sneaking into the saloon and having a quiet drink," he said.

"Don't know why that would bother you, Joe. I've never known you to do anything, quietly."

"You're the two gents who cut down Luke Grant, ain't you?" the bartender asked when they stepped up to the bar.

"I reckon that's us," Joe said.

"Then drink up, boys. The first one is on the house," he said. "What'll it be?"

Both boys ordered whiskey.

"Doesn't this town have any law?" Win asked, as he tossed the drink down.

"Yeah, we've got a town marshal," the bartender replied.

"Don't know what kind of marshal he is," Win said. "But I've not known many who just would stand by and watch a lynching."

"Oh, it wasn't a lynching," the bartender said. "Luke was hung all legal and proper."

"You're sayin' that was a legal hangin'?" Joe asked.

"Yes, sir. There may be some don't agree with it. Fact is, I don't agree with it. Far as I know, Luke Grant was an all right kind of man. He come in here a lot . . . was always quiet, and never give nobody any trouble."

"Then, how did he wind up trimming a tree?" Win asked.

"He went to Shelby and complained that some rustlers was stealin' his cows."

"Shelby?"

"Pete Shelby. He's the marshal," the bartender said. "Anyhow, Shelby said he would look in to it, but the next thing you know, ole' Luke was back in the marshal's office, claimin' that he just seen some of his cows bein' loaded onto the train cars. The marshal said he'd look into it, but Luke didn't want to wait. Instead, he just went down to the pens, opened the gates, and started herdin' the cows off . . . big as you please, in front of God and ever'body. The cattle buyers swore out a complaint against him, and Luke was tried for cattle rustling."

"You mean that's it? That's what they got him on?"

"Yes, sir. Well, they had him dead to rights," the bartender insisted. "I mean, the whole town seen him tryin' to take them cows."

"Seems to me like that would be more of a dispute over ownership than cattle rustling. And even if it was rustling, attempted cattle rustling is all they could really get him on," Joe said.

"Yes, sir, it does seem a shame. Like I said, Luke was just general well-liked around town."

''But nobody came to his defense?''

''What could anybody do? I mean, it ain't like he didn't do it.''

''What about the cattle he claimed were his? Anything done about that?''

''By the time the trial come around, them buyers had already shipped the cows out.''

Although Win was engaged in conversation with the bartender, he wasn't inattentive to what was going on behind him. In the mirror, he saw Harley come in. Harley made no attempt to approach them, but sat over in the corner instead, just watching.

''Do you know a man by the name of Truelove?'' Win asked.

''Otis Truelove? Sure, everyone 'round hear knows him. Is he a friend of yours?''

''An acquaintance,'' Win said. ''I heard he's had some trouble with rustlers, also.''

''I reckon he's had more trouble'n nearly anyone else. Some time back, three of his riders was found shot, and a lot of his cows was stole. Fact is, he had so many cows stole there's some folks bettin' he won't be able to make it much longer.''

''Excuse me for interruptin' the conversation here, barkeep,'' Joe said. ''But who is that rat-faced bastard sitting in the corner over there? I heard the others call him Harley. Harley who?'' Joe asked.

''His name is Harley Claymore. He's Doc Claymore's son.''

''Claymore's son?'' Joe said. Well, no wonder he took an interest in leaving Grant hanging from the tree. He was just lookin' out for papa's interest.''

''Who were the two toadies with him?'' Win asked.

''They're called Angus Spahn and Deekus Cain. Anytime you see Harley, you'll see them two, sucking up to 'im.''

''Some folks are hard-pressed for friends, I reckon,'' Joe said.

''Tell me about the rustlers who stole Truelove's cows. They ever find them?'' Win asked.

"No, sir. But the marshal has put up a pretty good reward for them. So has Doc Claymore."

"Claymore has put up a reward for the men who rustled Truelove's cattle? Why?" Win asked.

"Well, sir, the way Doc Claymore explains it, anyone who would rustle cows from one ranch, would rustle from any ranch. So he figures he's got as much at stake in gettin' the rustlers caught as Truelove."

"Makes sense, I suppose," Win said.

The bartender nodded, then held up the bottle. "You boys want another drink?"

Joe leaned across the bar. "Your whiskey is good, barkeep, but I was just wonderin' if maybe this town didn't have a few other things a man might need."

"I beg your pardon?"

"What my brother is talking about is women," Win explained. He looked around the saloon. "Come to think of it, I haven't seen any in here."

"Oh, there's a couple that hang around here, all right," he said. "But, by god, they are so ugly they'd make a train take ten miles of dirt road. Now, if you really want to find some women, you might want to check out Big Kate's Place."

"Big Kate's Place? Is that another saloon?" Joe asked.

"Saloon, my eye. Big Kate's Place is a whorehouse, gents. A genuine, first-class whorehouse, run by a lady called Big Kate. Fact is, it's also a fine hotel with good rooms as well as a café. And anyone will tell you, they set the finest table in town."

"And where might this place be?" Joe asked.

"It's a big, fine-lookin' white buildin' at the far end of town on the other side of the street. You can't miss it."

"What do you say, Win?" Joe asked. "You want to check it out?"

"We may as well," Win replied. The bartender had been about to pour them another drink, and he was still holding the bottle. "Tell you what, friend," Win said. "How about selling me the rest of that bottle you're holding in your hand?"

"It's about half-full; give me a dollar and it's yours," the bartender replied.

Win paid him, then he and Joe turned away from the bar and stared at Harley Claymore. Harley, remembering his last encounter with them, grabbed his hat and hurried out of the saloon. By the time the boys stepped out onto the front porch, Harley was mounted and riding quickly out of town.

Big Kate's Place was made of wood, two stories high, with a second-story balcony that ran all the way around the building. Below the balcony, at street level, was a fine wooden porch with a dozen rocking chairs. A very large, heavily painted woman got up from one of the chairs and smiled a greeting at the two brothers as they dismounted out front. She was smoking a cigar, and as she approached them she tapped off the ash at the end.

"Greetin's, gents. My name is Kathleen, but they call me Big Kate." Big Kate put her hand on a rather large hip, then gave it a bump, winking as she did so. "Don't have any idea why they call me that," she said.

Both boys laughed.

"You just visitin' the girls, or will you be takin' rooms?" Big Kate asked.

"Both," Joe answered.

"Well, if you're taking rooms, just leave your horses tied up there, and I'll have my man Clarence take care of 'em. We've got our own stables out back."

"That's nice," Joe said.

"Come on inside. I'll get you registered, and show you around."

The boys followed her through the double doors. For a place in such a small town, the lobby seemed huge. There were a dozen or more chairs and sofas scattered about, several potted plants, mirrors on the walls, and a grand, elegant staircase rising to the second floor.

"Will you be wantin' one room, or two?" Big Kate asked.

"We spend enough time together," Win said. "Whenever we can, we always take our own rooms."

"And we'd like them on the front, if you don't mind," Joe added. "We like a view."

Big Kate studied the two men for a minute. "You boys on the dodge? I don't want any trouble here."

"We're not wanted," Win said.

"But you have been, haven't you? Else, you wouldn't insist on a room where you can keep an eye on the town."

"Old habits die hard," Win said.

"All right, gents," Big Kate said. She took two keys down from a row of nails and handed one to each of them. "Right at the top of the stairs, one on the left and one on the right."

"Thanks."

"You got a place to take a bath in this hotel?" Joe asked, rubbing the stubble on his chin.

"Yes indeed," Big Kate said. She smiled proudly. "We even have a water tank on the roof so that we have running water."

While Big Kate was explaining how to get to the bathroom, Joe was looking around the lobby.

"Any more questions?" Big Kate asked.

"Yeah, where the hell are they?"

"I beg your pardon?"

"The girls? I thought this was a whorehouse."

"It is. There's not a better whorehouse within one hundred miles, if you ask me."

"Well?"

"Well, what?"

"Where are the whores?"

"Oh, I suspect most of them are sleeping. They work nights, you know."

"Can you roust one of them up?"

"Of course I can. Which one?"

Joe laughed. "Since I don't know any of them, it don't make no never mind to me. Just choose one. Choose the one you like the best."

Big Kate laughed, a deep, throaty laugh. "Well, now, honey, I like men, not women . . . so I don't have a favorite. But they are all fine-looking ladies, so I don't think you will be disappointed no matter who I select. I think I saw Kelly up and about a few minutes ago. I'll send her to your room."

"Fine, fine," Joe said, rubbing his hands together in anticipation. He turned to Win. "Big Brother, it looks like you are going to have to do without my company for a while."

"I'll manage," Win said. "I'll just take a look around and see what they have in this town."

Chapter 5

FIFTEEN MINUTES LATER JOE WAS IN THE BATHROOM, SET-
tled into the large brass bathtub. A clean shirt and clean pair
of pants hung over the back of a nearby chair. On the floor
beside him was half a glass of whiskey, and beside the glass,
what was left of the bottle he and Win had bought. A cigar
was elevated at a jaunty angle from his freshly shaved face,
and Joe was trying to wash his back while at the same time
singing, *"The dew is on the grass, Lorena . . ."*

His singing was interrupted by the sudden and unexpected
opening of the bathroom door. Grabbing his pistol, he brought
it up, thumbing back on the hammer as he did so.

"Oh!" the intruder gasped, frightened by the pistol.

"You ought not to scare a fella like that," Joe said.

"I scared you? What do you think you did to me?" A very
pretty young woman stepped into the room then, and closed
the door behind her. She had dark hair, green eyes, and dim-
ples.

"Uh, can I help you, miss?" Joe asked.

"No, but maybe I can help you. If you'll stop that infernal
racket, I'll wash your back for you." She knelt down beside
the tub, picked up the wash cloth, dipped it in the water, then
started running it down his back. "I'm Kelly Milhall. What's
your name?"

"Kelly, is it? Well, Kelly, my name is Joe Coulter. Are you
telling me you don't care for my singing?"

"Is that what you call it, Joe? I've heard coyotes do better," Kelly teased.

"Ah," Joe said in blissful appreciation. "A little more to the left. There, that's it. And, yes, I call it singing."

Joe sat silently for a minute as Kelly soaped his back a second time, then washed it off again.

"Do you provide this kind of service for all your customers?"

"No," Kelly said. "But I appreciate what you and your friend did for Mr. Grant."

"Mr. Grant?" Joe was confused for a moment. "Oh, you mean Luke Grant? The body we cut down?"

"Yes."

Joe sighed. "Don't think I'm not grateful for your appreciation, darlin', but cuttin' him down after he's already dead sure don't seem to me like we done much for him."

"Nevertheless, it was awful the way they let him just hang there. I could see him from the window in my room and I cried every time I looked."

"How well did you know him?"

"He was one of my regulars," Kelly said without shame. She dropped the washcloth, then reached around front, and down into the water. Grabbing him, she smiled at him. "Are we just going to talk all day? Or do you have something else in mind?"

Joe sucked in a gasping breath. "As a matter of fact, I do have something else in mind," he said.

Kelly kissed him then. Her mouth opened and their tongues met. She began moving her hand back and forth on the hard shaft of his penis. That was when Joe suddenly stood up. She looked at him with confusion on her face, surprised by his sudden move.

"I'll be damned if I'm going to do this in a bathtub," he said. "Let's go down to my room."

Joe strapped on his pistol belt and put on his hat. Then, unembarrassed by his nakedness, he walked down the hall with Kelly, carrying his clothes and boots. Once in the room, he put his clothes down, then pulled her body hard against his, meeting her with another kiss. She opened her mouth hungrily to seek out his tongue. Joe's arms wound around her tightly, then Kelly pulled away from him.

"What's wrong?" Joe asked.

"You aren't planning to be wearing that when we do it, are you?" Kelly asked with a giggle, pointing to the pistol belt.

"Uh, no, I guess not," he said. He unstrapped the belt, then hooked it over the bedstead, letting it hang in a way that would allow him quick access to the pistol.

"And that?" Kelly said, pointing to the hat.

"What about you?" Joe said as he took off his hat. "You going to get out of your clothes?"

Kelly stepped back from him and, as she studied him through smoky eyes, began removing her dress, garment by garment, until she stood before him as naked as he.

"You like what you see?" she asked, turning and posturing before him.

"Too damned much talk," Joe said, pulling her to him. He felt her naked breasts mash against his bare chest as they kissed again, then he picked her up and deposited her on the bed. He climbed on top, and she threw her arms around his neck, wriggling and squirming beneath him. She spread her legs to receive him, and when he entered her, he felt her buck with the sudden rush of pleasure.

"Yes," she said, matching her rhythms to his in eager counterpoint.

Kelly's skin was soft and as hot as if burning with fever. Even though she was a working girl, it was obvious that she was deriving a great deal of pleasure from this.

Finally, Joe could hold back no longer and he burst inside her. Kelly felt it, and she cried out with the pleasure of it and clasped him tightly to her as if unwilling to let him go.

Sated at last, Joe collapsed atop her, until his breathing returned to normal.

He felt good.

He let out a sigh and rolled off her, then lay beside her, listening to the receding sound of her raspy breathing, touching her soft belly.

"Thank you, Joe," she whispered.

Joe raised up on one elbow and looked down at her. The

breasts were generous pillows, the nipples, hard and erect. Joe reached down to touch one, and she shivered in pleasure.

"You ought not to do that," she said.

"Why not?"

"Because you'll be starting something you can't finish."

Joe chuckled, then moved her hand down to feel him. "Who said I can't finish it?" he asked.

At one time, Marshal Pete Shelby had been a pretty good lawman. As a member of the St. Louis police department, he had been cited for finding, and bringing to justice the River Front Murderer. But that was fifteen years ago. Now, he was overage and overweight. He was the town marshal, not the county sheriff. That meant his authority extended only to the town limits, a fact he pointed out every time someone suggested he should go after Potter and his outlaws.

Shelby bemoaned the fact that he had no authority beyond the town limits, but in truth, he was glad he didn't have to be put to the test. He could still handle drunks and barroom fights. That was enough to satisfy both the mandate of his office and the dictates of his conscience.

Until the incident with Luke Grant, Shelby believed that he had enjoyed the support of most of the citizen of the county. And even the incident with Grant could be justified. Grant had clearly violated the law. He stole cattle from the loading pens. Nearly a dozen people in town saw him do it.

All Shelby did was arrest him. After that, the law took its course. Grant was given a fair trial, found guilty, and sentenced to hang by the circuit judge. Everything was legal and above board.

It had been Claymore's idea to leave the body hanging as a warning against other cattle thieves. But even that violated no laws, though it did offend Shelby's sense of what was right and wrong. And, he told himself, maybe Claymore was right. Maybe it would serve as a warning to cattle thieves, though it seemed obvious to Shelby that Luke Grant's situation was different. He clearly wasn't one of the thieves who had been plaguing the county.

Shelby contemplated these things as he stood in his office.

He was drinking a cup of coffee and looking through the window, down Front Street.

Harley Claymore had come in earlier, protesting the fact that Win and Joe Coulter had attacked him, Spahn, and Cain, out in the street last night.

"From what I hear, you boys confronted them," Shelby said. "So, what do you want me to do about it? Arrest them for beating you up? I'll do it if you want me to, but folks are sure to get a laugh out of it."

"No. I can handle my own fights," Harley replied. "But somethin' ought to be done about them cuttin' Luke Grant's body down." Harley came over to stand beside Shelby. When he happened to look out the window, he saw Win walking up the sidewalk. "Hey, there's one of them now! Do you see him?"

"I see him," Shelby answered calmly.

"Well, what are you going to do about it?"

"What do you propose that I do about it?" Shelby asked, turning toward Harley. "All they did was cut down a body that had been hanging from a tree for two days. That's not breaking any law that I know of."

"Ain't you got no paper on them? I heard people talking about them. Their name is Coulter, Win and Joe Coulter. They rode with Quantrill during the war. I heard near 'bout all them is wanted men now."

"That may be true, but they aren't wanted in my town," Shelby said.

"Damn! He's comin' in here!" Harley said, realizing then that Win was headed straight for the marshal's office. Harley looked around quickly. "I . . . I'd better scoot out the back. It wouldn't look good for him to see us together."

"You can go down the alley," Shelby said. He watched, barely able to contain a smile, as Harley sneaked out of the back door.

The front door opened a moment later and Win Coulter stepped inside.

"You the marshal, or the deputy?" Win asked.

"I'm Marshal Shelby, Mr. Coulter. I don't have a deputy.

The town budget doesn't allow for one. What can I do for you?''

It didn't surprise Win that the marshal knew who he was. On the contrary, he would have been surprised if the Marshal hadn't known. With the reputation he and his brother had developed, he had grown to expect to be known by the lawman of just about every town they visited.

"Where can I find Doc Claymore?" Win asked

"What do you want with him?" he asked.

"He's the biggest cattleman around here, isn't he?"

"That's right."

"Then I need to talk to him."

"You sure you want to do that? Cuttin' ole Luke Grant down from that tree like you and your brother done won't sit none too well with Doc Claymore. Not only that, you beat up his son."

"That's true, but I still want to talk to him."

"Are you the law?" Shelby asked.

"In a manner of speaking."

"What do you mean, in a manner of speaking?"

"There is a reward being offered for bringing in the rustlers killed Truelove's men, isn't there?"

"Yes."

"Then, in a manner of speaking, anyone who goes out after that reward is working for the law."

Shelby studied Win through squinted eyes. "I never would have believed this," he said. "Are you telling me you and your brother are bounty hunters?"

"It's not what I would call our profession. But we are going after the rustlers who killed Truelove's men."

"You and your brother are welcome to try, of course, but I'm afraid you will find that it's not all that simple. People around here have been looking for Potter and his bunch for nearly two years now. What makes you think you can find 'em, when no one else has been able to?"

"Because we generally do what we set out to do," Win answered. "Now, where is Claymore?"

"His ranch starts about five miles north of here. You can't

miss it. Once you get there, it stretches for as far as you can see in any direction.''

"Thanks," Win said, starting toward the door.

"Coulter?" Shelby called.

"Yes?" Win turned back toward the Marshal.

"Outside the town limits, you and your brother can poke around all you want. But when you are in town, don't forget who the real law is around here.''

"Well, now, seems to me like that's the question, isn't it?" Win replied. "Just who *is* the real law around here?"

"By god, I am," Shelby said, in a blustering answer.

"Is that a fact? Does Claymore know that?" Win asked.

Chapter 6

ONE OF THE AMENITIES THE CUSTOMERS COULD ENJOY AT BIG Kate's was a friendly game of cards. On the wall there was a sign which read: THIS IS AN HONEST GAMBLING ESTABLISHMENT. PLEASE REPORT ANY CHEATING TO THE MANAGEMENT.

In addition to the self-righteous claim of gambling integrity, the walls were also decorated with game-heads and pictures, including one of a reclining nude woman. Some marksman had already added his own improvement to the painting by putting three holes through the woman in all the appropriate places, though one shot had missed the target, slightly, giving her left breast two nipples. There was no gilt-edged mirror, but there was an ample supply of decent whiskey, and several large jars of pickled eggs and sausages placed in convenient locations.

By the time Win returned to Big Kate's Place, all the girls were up and tending to business. Win saw one of the girls taking a cowboy up the stairs with her.

The upstairs area didn't extend all the way to the front of the building. The main room, or salon, was big, with exposed rafters below the high, peaked ceiling. The "grand" salon, as Big Kate insisted upon calling it, was almost like a private club. There were a score or more customers present, sitting on the sofa or in big easy chairs, talking with the girls, drinking, or playing cards.

Big Kate came over to Win, then put her arm through his.

"Welcome back, Mr. Coulter," she said. "I trust you had a productive day as you wandered around our little town."

"It was all right," Win said. He looked around the salon. "Where is my brother?"

Big Kate laughed. "Let's just say that your brother's day has been equally productive, though perhaps in a different arena. Could I get you something to drink, Mr. Coulter?"

"Yes," Win said.

"Wine, beer, or whiskey?"

"Whiskey," Win said.

"Linda, do keep Mr. Coulter company while I get him something to drink," Big Kate said, adroitly putting Win with one of her girls. Linda was heavily painted and showed the dissipation of her profession. There was no humor or life left to her eyes, and when Win didn't appear to show too much interest in her, she turned and walked over to sit by the piano player.

The piano player wore a small, round derby hat and kept his sleeves up with garter belts. He was pounding out a rendition of "Buffalo Gals," though the music was practically lost amidst the noise of a dozen or more conversations.

"Oh, my, you didn't like Linda?" Big Kate asked, returning with Win's whiskey.

"Linda was fine," Win said. He put his arm around as much of Big Kate as he could. "But after being greeted by you, everyone else seems second rate."

Big Kate laughed out loud. "My, my, Mr. Coulter, you do have a golden tongue," she said. "But you had better be careful who you flirt with. I might decide you're serious. Oh, excuse me, some more customers just came in."

Big Kate left Win standing alone in the middle of the salon, smiling and drinking his whiskey.

One of the customers, a young cowboy, got up and walked over to Win, carrying his beer with him.

"Hello, Win. I heard you and Joe were in town."

"Ev Butrum, isn't it?" Win asked. "Last time I saw you was in San Angelo, I believe."

"You've got a good memory," Butrum said.

"Still trying to fill an inside straight?" Win asked, recalling a card game they once played.

"Haven't had any more luck with that here than I did back there," Ev answered with a chuckle.

"What are you doing in these parts?" Win asked.

"Trying to make a dollar. I've hired on with Mr. Truelove."

Win took a drink, studying Butrum over the rim of the glass. "Is that a fact? I heard Truelove had a little trouble there a while ago."

"You got that right. Three of our men were killed, and a couple hundred head of cows were stolen."

"You have any idea of who did it?" Win asked.

"Hell yes, I know who did it. Everyone knows who did it."

"Emil Potter?" Win asked.

"You know about him?"

"I've heard the name, that's all."

"Potter and a band of outlaws have a hideout somewhere in the hills nearby. Nobody's been able to find out just where. Or, if anyone has, they've not lived to tell about it. What brings you and Joe to town?"

"A man's got to be somewhere," Win replied.

"I hear you might be going after Potter, for the bounty."

"Where'd you hear that?"

"I was talking to Marshal Shelby."

"Well, if a bounty falls in our lap, we won't walk away from it," Win replied.

"If you're goin' to get involved, I think you should know that we practically have a range war going on between the rustlers and the ranchers. You could be bitin' off more'n you bargained for."

"Wouldn't be the first time we wandered into a hornets' nest," Win said.

Ev nodded. "Yeah," he said. "Well, I didn't figure you'd just pull up stakes and go away. But don't say you wasn't warned."

"Win, open the door," Joe called the next morning.

Win opened his eyes and looked around. A bright morning

sun was streaming in through the open window. He heard Joe
call out again, this time augmenting his call, by banging on
the door.

"Win, you awake in there?"

"Yeah," Win said. He got out of bed, yawned and
stretched, then padded over to the door in his bare feet and
opened it. He stepped back to let his brother in.

"You tryin' to wake the dead?" Win complained.

"You planning' on sleepin' all day?" Joe countered, barg-
ing into the room. He walked over to the window and put it
all the way up. "You need some air in here. No wonder you
were still asleep. It's stuffy."

"What time is it?"

"Damn near six-thirty," Joe replied. "Half the day is gone
already."

"Oh, well, hell, what was I thinking, laying up 'til near
noon like that?" Win replied sarcastically. He went over to
the basin and began brushing his teeth. He had no toothpaste,
so he used whiskey.

"I love the smell when the morning sun hits the fresh piles
of horse shit in the street, don't you?" Joe asked. He took a
deep breath.

Win chuckled. "You're crazy, Little Brother, you know
that?" he said. "And I don't know where you get it from,
'cause I know it didn't run in the family."

Joe turned away from the window. "Win, didn't you say
you wanted to ride out to Claymore Ranch today?" Joe asked.

"Yeah, I thought it might be time we meet this fella face-
to-face."

"There's no need to go out to his ranch to do that."

"What do you mean?"

"He's coming to a meeting of the Cattlemen's Association."

Win began working up a shaving lather. "Maybe we ought
to try and get ourselves an invite to the meeting," he suggested.

"We've already been invited. By Otis Truelove."

"You've been to see Truelove?"

"Didn't have to go see him. He's downstairs right now," Joe said. "Waiting to have breakfast with us, in fact."

Truelove was in the salon having coffee with Big Kate when Win and Joe came down the stairs. He stood to greet them.

"When Ev Butrum told me you two men were here, I didn't believe him," he said. "But here you are, in the flesh. It's good to see you boys." He smiled at Win. "Still carrying water to your wounded enemies?" he asked.

"Not so much, these days," Win said. "It's become more difficult to find honorable enemies."

"Ain't that the damned truth?" Truelove agreed.

"Gentlemen, I've set a table, just for you," Big Kate said. "This way."

Big Kate led them, not into the main dining room, but to a smaller, much more elegant, and more private room. A breakfast buffet was laid out for them, and the men moved through slowly, filling their plates.

"What brings you boys to Paso del Muerte?" Truelove asked.

"You," Win said.

Truelove looked at him in surprise.

"Me? How so?"

"Or rather, what happened on your ranch a month or so ago."

"You mean about my three riders getting killed? Yes, that was really a shame. Look here, Win, did you know any of them?"

"No. I heard about Billy Goodwin from his sister, Irene," Win said. "She tried to hire Joe and me to look into it."

"How is Irene getting along?"

"She seems to be doing just fine."

"After Billy was killed, I tried to get Irene to move over here," Truelove said. "I told her I could get her fixed up with Big Kate. But, she's got friends over there. And she said she didn't want to have anything to do with a town that could let an innocent boy like her brother get killed, and do nothing about it." Truelove looked across the table at Win. "You say she tried to hire you? No need of her spendin' her money to find out who killed my men. Tell me what she offered, and I'll pay it.''

''I told her we didn't want her money,'' Win said.

''Too bad you aren't interested.''

''I didn't say we weren't interested,'' Win said. ''I just said I didn't want to take her money. From what I hear, there is already a reward posted.''

''There is, but rewards are pretty iffy things. On the other hand, I have a proposal that might interest you. How would you like to work for the Cattlemen's Association? I'm sure they would be willing to compensate you generously.''

''Joe told me you had invited us to attend the meeting today. Will Doc Claymore be there?'' Win asked.

''Claymore? Yes, he'll be there. He's president of the association. I'm the vice-president.''

''Claymore might not be in a hiring mood,'' Joe suggested. ''Particularly as we cut down his tree decoration.''

Truelove chuckled. ''You let me handle Claymore. He's frustrated, like all the rest of us. I'm telling you, Potter and his rustlers are worse than a plague of locusts. He's already run a couple of good ranchers out of business, and he has hurt us all, Claymore included.''

''All right, Mr. Truelove,'' Win said. ''We'll apply for the job.''

With Truelove as their sponsor, Win and Joe were invited into the inner sanctum of the Cattlemen's Association. Some of the men, Win noticed, had been at Big Kate's Place the night before, and though they nodded at each other in recognition of the fact that they had seen each other there, no one spoke of it.

As Truelove had promised, Doc Claymore was present for the meeting. He was fairly small man, with curly gray hair, dark, beady eyes, a narrow mouth, and a nose which was shaped somewhat like a hawk's beak.

In addition to Truelove and Claymore, there were four other men present. They were dressed as businessmen, but Win saw immediately that they would have been much more comfortable dressed exactly as he and Joe were. The ranchers were used to the saddle and to range clothes, and they pulled at their collars and tugged at their sleeves.

Doc Claymore was more formally dressed than any of the other ranchers, wearing a three-piece suit and a silk shirt, with a diamond stick-pin in his tie. As the wealthiest man in the territory, Doc Claymore was a natural for the position of president of the Paso del Muerte Cattleman's Association.

Other men might have felt intimidated by this display of ostentation, but Win and Joe were neither impressed nor intimidated. Instead, they sat there listening to Otis Truelove as he made his pitch to the board.

"I think I can speak for all the cattlemen when I say that we have come to the conclusion that desperate measures are needed to stop the terrible plague of rustling we have been experiencing," Truelove said.

"I'll say. If this goes on any longer, it's going to drive me out of business," one of the other ranchers said. He was a big man with a sweeping moustache.

"Yeah, and not only Hardin here, but me and Vogel and Masters too," another added.

"Do you want the floor, Mr. Baker?" Claymore asked the one who was speaking.

"Well, yeah, I guess. I mean, hell, I thought I already had the floor," Baker replied.

"You don't have the floor until the chair says you have the floor," Claymore explained. He cleared his throat, then made a show of announcing: "The chair now recognizes George Baker." Claymore looked at the others. "Let's keep this in order. If we are going to spend money to hire a couple of men, then everything has to be above board. All right, George, you may speak."

"Thanks," Baker said. "I guess we all know that Doc Claymore is about the only one stout enough to keep going. In fact when the rustlers hit me really hard a couple months ago, it was Doc Claymore that loaned me the money I needed to make a note at the bank. If it wasn't for him I don't know what I would do."

"At least you're tryin'," Vogel said. "Montgomery and Hughes just chucked it in and went back home."

Doc Claymore leaned back in his chair and sighed. "I'm afraid the truth is they were too small to even try it out here. Of course, their instinct was to fight back, but when the rustlers started hitting them, they didn't have anything to fight with. They weren't left with enough cattle to even make all the ends meet, and they went under."

"It could've been worse," Baker said.

"How could it have been worse?" Vogel asked. "Neither one of them are here anymore."

"It could've been worse because they might have had to go back East with nothing. As it is, they at least had enough money to get them back."

"Yeah, you're right. Thanks to Doc Claymore buyin' them out, they didn't leave here completely broke," Vogel agreed.

"You mean you have their ranches now?" Win asked, raising his eyebrows.

"Yes."

"I see."

"No, Mr. Coulter, I don't think you do see," Baker interjected. "Doc Claymore didn't *have* to buy them out. Hell, once they abandoned their ranches the land was out there, just for the taking. Doc Claymore paid them for it when, by law, he didn't have to pay them a cent."

"I couldn't just take over," Doc Claymore said. "I wouldn't have felt good about that. After all, both men did have families to support."

"He's made the same standing offer to the rest of us," Baker said. "And I have to confess that knowing he will buy us out if need be gives us a little more incentive to try and get something done."

"It could also make you less willing to stand and fight, figuring you can always sell out and leave," Joe suggested.

"Yeah, well, I'm not ready to leave just yet," the rancher named Hardin said. "So, I'm willin' to see what it is you boys can offer us."

Hardin took two cigars from his jacket pocket and gave one to Win and the other to Joe. They accepted, and after biting off the ends, waited for Hardin to provide the match. Hardin lit both of them and they were able to take several puffs before Claymore spoke up.

"I understand you two boys had a run-in with my son last night," he finally said.

"We had a little difference of opinion on that cottonwood tree that stands down there, next to the depot. Harley and his friends thought it should be decorated. My brother and I thought it shouldn't."

Doc Claymore chuckled. "I'll say this for you two boys. You settled it pretty fast. They tell me you're called the Bushwhackers," Claymore said. "That's what they called the men who rode with Quantrill, isn't it? Bushwhackers?"

"Not just Quantrill. The name generally applied to any Missourian who was caught up in the border war with Kansas."

"Is that what it was? A border war?" Claymore asked.

Win took a puff of his cigar, then, with squinted eyes, stared through the smoke at Claymore. "Yes," he finally said after a pause that was so long that the others were beginning to think he wasn't going to speak at all. "It was a border war."

"Did you men ride with Quantrill?"

"We did."

"So they rode with Quantrill. What's your point, Claymore?" Truelove finally asked.

"It's funny that you, of all people, would have to ask me that, Truelove," Claymore replied. "You were an officer in the Union Army, weren't you? You know what kind of men Quantrill's riders were. Besides, why am I having to explain this to you, or to anyone?"

"I know what kind of man Quantrill was," Truelove said. He nodded toward Win and Joe. "But I also know what kind of man each of these men were. They conducted themselves with honor then, and I see no reason to think otherwise of them now."

"Yes, well, it's not just their wartime experiences that I'm talking about," Claymore said. He looked at Win and Joe. "I have heard of your exploits since the war's end. In fact, a lot of people have. You two have the reputation of leaving a lot of dead men in your wake."

"We've left our share of dead," Win admitted. "But we've never killed unless it was a time for killing."

"I see," Claymore said. "And, who decides when it is a time for killing."

"We decide when it is time for killing," Joe said. Joe's words fell upon the room with the impact of pistol shots.

"Hell, that's fine with me," Baker suddenly said. "Truth is, we want you two to hunt the rustlers down. We want you to hunt them down and when you find them, we want you to kill them on the spot."

Win took the cigar out of his mouth and studied the end of it for a moment before he looked up at Baker.

"It's like my brother said, Mr. Baker. *We* are the ones who will decide when it's time for killing," Win said. "But we don't kill on command, and we're not professional executioners."

Baker raised his eyebrows. "You're squeamish about killing?"

"Not at all. As I said, we have killed when it was necessary. But unnecessary killing is a waste of time and energy."

"If you ask me, it's bringing these sons of biches in to be tried that is a waste of time and energy," Vogel said. "Why don't you just kill 'em, and be done with it?"

Win stood up and put his cigar down on the ashtray.

"You gents don't want us. You want a couple of assassins. You can get someone else."

Doc Claymore began clapping his hands slowly, as if applauding a performance.

"Bravo," he said. "Bravo, Mr. Coulter." Doc Claymore smiled at the other members of the organization. "Gentlemen, if I had any doubts about these men before, I have none now."

"What is this?" Win asked.

"Well, my dear fellow, when I agreed with these gentlemen to discuss hiring outside help, I had certain reservations. I wasn't sure just how far you would go. I was concerned that if we gave you *carte blanche* you might unleash a bloodbath in our fair valley." He smiled at Win and Joe. "But, after listening to you talk, I now believe that you are men of integrity and ethics. Most of all, you are men with a sense of values.

I can, in all good conscience, employ your services, and know that there will not be a sudden onslaught of wanton killing. Gentlemen, you are hired.''

"We're not hired, unless we say we are hired," Win said. He picked the cigar up again. "Now, we have a few questions of our own, if you don't mind."

"But of course you do," Doc Claymore said. "I imagine the first thing you want to know is what will be your pay?"

"That's a start," Win said.

"Yes. Well, I propose that we pay you two hundred fifty dollars per month, plus a bonus of two hundred fifty dollars for every cattle thief you eliminate by, uh, whatever method is needed, regardless of the reward that is currently in effect. In addition, you will receive whatever government award is in effect, whether more or less. And when you bring in their leader, Emil Potter, we will pay you one thousand dollars. Not only that, you can begin drawing your money immediately. We are prepared to give you a two-hundred-fifty-dollar advance."

"The money sounds reasonable enough," Win agreed.

"You will, of course, be required to report in to us often," Baker said. "We want to know what is going on."

"No, we won't do that," Win said.

"Why not?" Hardin asked.

"You ever heard the story of putting a bell on a cat?" Win asked. "If we have to report in here to you people, the outlaws will always have an idea of where we are."

"But look here! This is ridiculous," Baker sputtered. "We can't be expected to pay you two this kind of money and then have absolutely no idea as to where you are, no control over where you go or what you do."

"That's the way it's going to be," Win said.

"Of course it is," Otis Truelove said. He looked at the others. "Listen to me, gentlemen. I say we need these two men. And if the only way we can employ them is to hire them on their own terms, then I don't see that we have any choice but to comply."

There was grumbling exchange of conversation for a moment or two, then Hardin spoke up.

"All right," he said. "If Otis here is satisfied with them, then I am too."

Hardin's acquiescence brought on agreement from all the others, including Doc Claymore, who then renewed the negotiations.

"You can operate any way you want, come and go as you like. The only thing we want is for these damn rustlers to be eliminated. Because if they aren't wiped out, and wiped out fast, there may not be any cattlemen left in this entire valley."

Win relit his cigar, smiled at them, then he and Joe started for the door.

"Wait!" Claymore called. "Are you going to take the job?"

Without looking around, Win held his cigar up and nodded.

"When will we hear from you again?"

"When we come for our money," Win replied.

Chapter 7

IT HAD BEEN THREE DAYS SINCE WIN AND JOE AGREED TO take the job, and two nights since several cows were stolen from Vogel's herd. Last night the rustlers hit again, taking cows from Baker's herd.

Angered, Baker called a meeting at his house of all the ranchers in the valley.

As the nearby mountains turned from red to purple in the setting sun, Baker's friends and neighbors began arriving for the meeting. Wagons and buggies brought entire families across the range to gather at the Baker house. Children who lived too far apart to play with each other laughed and squealed and ran from wagon to wagon to greet their friends before dashing off to a twilight game of kick-the-can. The women, who had brought cakes and pies from home, gathered in the kitchen to make coffee, thus turning the business meeting into a great social event. Many of them brought quilts and they spread them out so that, while the men were meeting, they could work on the elaborate colors and patterns of the quilts they would be displaying at the next fair.

The cowboys were invited too. They had an interest in the proceedings, for if the ranchers lost their ranches, the cowboys would lose their jobs. However, the cowboys were working hands and they didn't feel comfortable around the ranchers and their families, so most of them declined, respectfully.

Doc Claymore attended the meeting, accompanied by his

son, Harley. Harley went straight to the sideboard for a glass
of whiskey.

Truelove was the last rancher to show up. He came in a
buckboard, accompanied by his wife, Martha, and his daughter, Lucy. Lucy was, according to all the cowboys, by far the
prettiest young woman on the range. Harley had made a few
overtures toward Lucy and many believed they would even-
tually wind up together.

"No way a pretty woman like that is going to marry a no-
count like Harley Claymore," some of the more adamant of
the cowboys protested. "There's no way she could love him."

"Love has nothing to do with it," the more pragmatic of
the cowboys pointed out. "Besides, Doc Claymore is all right.
Harley is just spoiled, that's all. He's spoiled 'cause he grew
up rich. But he'll come around."

When Truelove arrived Harley was standing on the porch.
He hurried out to offer his assistance to Lucy as she stepped
down from the buckboard. She smiled at him, being very careful to make the smile one of courtesy, and not invitation. Once
inside, Lucy hurried back to the kitchen to join the women.

"Let's get the meetin' goin'," Baker suggested.

The Truelove Ranch was three miles south of the Baker ranch,
where the meeting was being held. Because Truelove had not
yet replaced the three men who had been killed, there were
only four cowboys still working at his place, and, they, like
the cowboys from all the other ranches, had been invited to
the meeting. But also, like many of the cowboys from the other
ranches, they had declined.

At this very moment, one of the four men was cooking
supper for all of them, while the other three were sitting
around a scarred table, playing cards. Ev Butrum was dealing,
and they were only playing for matches, but that didn't lessen
the intensity of their game. When one of them took the pot
with a pair of aces, Ev complained.

"Pete! You son of a bitch! Where'd you get that ace?"
Ev's oath was softened by a burst of laughter.

"Don't you know? I took it from Shorty's boot when he
wasn't lookin' a while ago." Shorty was the third player.

"Does Shorty keep an ace in his boot?"

"You think he don't? I never know'd him to do anythin' honest when he could cheat."

"That's the truth," Shorty answered laconically. "But don't let Pete fool you none, Ev. Only reason he took mine was 'cause he'd already used his."

"What are you men doing? Trying to make a career of cheating?"

"I admit I practice it a little," Shorty said. "If I ever get real good at it, I'm goin' to take me a train out to San Francisco and find a real game with real tables an' win my fortune."

"Or get your lights put out for good," Ev Butrum replied. "Cheatin' your friends for matches is one thing. Cheatin' in a real game is liable to get a fella killed."

The cards were raked in, the deck shuffled, then re-dealt.

"You think all them ranchers is goin' to come up with anythin' at this meetin' they got goin' on over to the Baker place?" Shorty asked.

"I don't know. If they don't, they're all goin' to go out of business and me an' you an' Pete an' Troy is all goin' to be lookin' for jobs somewhere else."

"Maybe we could wind up workin' for Doc Claymore," Shorty suggested. "Seem's like ever'time someone quits ranchin', he takes over."

"Yeah, but if you notice, he don't hire all the cowboys from the old ranch. Hell, he don't even hire half of 'em. The rest of 'em is left out in the cold," Pete said.

"Yeah, that's true," Shorty agreed.

"What I'm hopin' is that them two fellas they hired will stop the rustlin'," Ev went on.

"I don't know. That seems like a pretty big job for just two men," Troy said.

"The Coulters aren't just ordinary men. I know, because I've run across them before."

Ev looked over at the man who was cooking their supper. He smiled, and waved his hand in the front of his nose. "What the hell is that you're cookin' over there, anyhow, Troy? Some dead skunk you found out on the trail?"

"Listen, you don't want to eat it, you can always rustle up your own supper," Troy replied, stirring the pot.

"Hell, I didn't say I wasn't goin' to eat it," Ev answered. "It's your bet, Shorty. You in or out?" he asked impatiently. Then, to Troy he called, "I just said it stinks, that's all."

"I can't bet more'n one match," Shorty said. "Pete took my ace." He slid a match into the little pile in the middle of the table.

"Whoa! One whole match!" Ev teased. "Well, I'll just raise you five matches." Ev looked over at Troy. "What I aim to do is win all the matches so Troy can't start no more fires in that stove. Then we won't have to worry none about his cookin', or our bein' poisoned."

"Ev, you're as full of shit as a Christmas goose," Shorty said. "Don't pay no never mind to him, Troy," he said over his shoulder to the cook. "You know him. He'd eat the north end of a southbound mule while the mule was still walkin'."

Outside the bunkhouse, six riders stopped on a little hill overlooking the ranch and ground-tied their mounts. They crept to the edge of the hill, crouched down, then looked down toward the bunkhouse.

"Looks like they's four of them here," one of the men said. "I can see 'em through the window. Three of 'em's sittin' at a table and another one is standin' up."

"Don't matter how many is here. Potter said kill 'em all, so let's commence shootin'. You three, aim at the one that's sittin' on the left and the one standin'. Me and Johnny and Poke will take the other two."

"I'm ready," Johnny replied.

All four men raised their rifles and took slow, careful aim. Their targets were well illuminated by the lantern that burned brightly inside the bunkhouse.

"Shoot!" the little group's leader said, squeezing the trigger that sent out the first bullet.

Suddenly Troy let out a little grunt of pain, spun around once, then fell to the floor.

"What the hell you doin'?" Shorty asked, laughing at what he thought was a joke.

"Boys, I been shot!" Troy gasped.

The laughter died in Shorty's throat as bullets began crashing through the glass windows and popping through the thin board walls, smashing crockery, careening off the iron stove, and projecting lead splinters and shards of glass like miniature bursts of shrapnel.

"My God! My God! What is it? What's happening?" Pete shouted.

"Get down!" Ev shouted. He dropped to the floor and crawled over to the window while bullets continued to crash and whiz through the little shack. When he looked out the window, he saw three men with rifles hiding behind the watering trough, firing at the bunkhouse. There were another three over behind the stable fence.

"Rustlers!" Ev yelled, but there was no one left to hear him. When he looked back inside, he saw that the other three were already dead.

Ev knew he had to get out of there, or he would be dead, too. The walls of the bunkhouse were too thin to stop the bullets. The only protection they could offer would be to mask Ev's movement. Using that to his advantage, Ev managed to tear out a couple of floor boards. As soon as the hole was big enough, he crawled through it to the ground below the cabin.

He felt the dank coolness of the dirt, smelled its odor, and breathed a small prayer of thanks that he had come this far without being hit. Whoever was shooting at the cabin did not realize that Ev had slipped away, for the bullets continued to crash through the cabin overhead with the intensity of a heavy hail.

Lifting up his head just enough to see where he was going, Ev slithered on his belly to the back of the bunkhouse, then rolled down into a small depression that allowed him to move, undetected, several feet away. Here, he was able to let himself down into a gully that was deep enough for him to stand. Once there, he started running without looking back, until the gunfire behind him sounded no more ominous than corn popping on a stove.

• • •

Win and Joe were camping at least two miles away from the ranch when they heard the shooting. Because of the echo, however, they couldn't be sure of the direction the shooting was coming from. Win climbed to the top of a large rock outcropping while the firing was still going on to see if he could find out. Then, far to the west, he saw a series of winking lights and knew that they were muzzle flashes.

"It's Truelove's place," Win said.

Joe was already extinguishing the camp fire. Win jumped down from the rock and within a couple of minutes both horses were saddled and the camp was broken.

Back at the meeting at the Baker Ranch, the ranchers were complaining bitterly over the fact that rustling was still going on.

"It's time we did something about it," Vogel said.

"We did do something about it. We hired the Coulter brothers," Truelove replied.

"The Coulters ain't done shit."

"Give 'em time."

Baker held up his hands to quiet the group, then he nodded toward Doc Claymore, who had been watching and listening to the whole thing. So far, Doc Claymore had said nothing.

"I think maybe Doc Claymore might have a suggestion or two for us," Baker said.

At Baker's invitation, Claymore stood up to address the other men who were gathered there.

"Gentlemen, what we need," he began, "is to form a corporation. A cattle corporation."

"What do you mean?" Vogel asked.

"Yeah, how would something like that work?"

"It's really very simple," Doc Claymore explained. "We would merge all of our ranches and our cattle into one large cattle company. We would each own a share of the company, in proportion with what we put into it."

"What would be the advantage of such a thing?" Truelove wanted to know.

Claymore started to answer, then he saw the wood box sitting by the stove. Though the stove was cool now, the wood box was full, including the smaller sticks used for kindling. Claymore reached down and picked up a few of them.

"When you're gatherin' sticks for a fire," Claymore said, "have you ever noticed how easy it is to break one stick?" He snapped a single twig. "But put several of them together and you can't break them, no matter how hard you try." He demonstrated his point by putting several of the sticks together.

"That works with sticks," Truelove said. "But I need a more practical answer."

"All right, how about this for an answer?" Claymore went on. "Suppose you put five-hundred head into the corporation and say, two hundred and fifty head were stolen. You wouldn't, personally, be out two hundred and fifty head. You would be out only a portion of that two hundred and fifty head, because the rest of us would absorb the loss with you."

"If they are his cows, why should the rest of us lose anything?" Masters asked.

"Because, we'd all be partners in this thing," Claymore answered. "We would share in each others' adversity and in each others' success. We would be like brothers."

"That sounds pretty good," Vogel agreed. "If you put it that way, then I'm for it."

"Yeah, me too," Masters added.

"Well, it looks like it's up to you, Truelove. What do you say?" Baker asked.

"I don't know," Truelove replied. "It might be hard, going it alone. But I'm not ready to give up my own ranch and start riding for Doc Claymore."

"It wouldn't be that way," Claymore said. "You won't be working for me. You'll be like all the other owners, a partner in a ranch that is bigger than anything you've ever dreamed of."

"What about the men we'd need to work an outfit this large?" Truelove asked. "Who would they be workin' for? Me, or this big ranch? I've only got four hands left, and I sort of hate losing control over them."

"They'd still be your men."

"You say that. But when it comes right down to it, somebody's goin' to have to be the boss, right?" Truelove asked.

"Yes, of course," Doc Claymore replied. "You would have anarchy otherwise. We could make the election of a president our first priority."

"I agree," Vogel said. "I say we elect the president now. Anyone got any ideas who it should be?"

"I say we elect Doc Claymore," Baker proposed.

"I second that," Masters said.

"He's got my vote," Vogel put in.

"Truelove, it's up to you, now," Baker said.

"I'd like some time to think about it."

"Time? Man, we're runnin' out of time! The rustlers is bleedin' us white!" Baker said.

Suddenly someone burst through the front door, startling everyone with his unexpected entrance. His clothes were dirty and torn. His face was scratched by brush, his hat was gone, and he was bent over with his hands on his knees, breathing hard.

"Mr. Truelove! Mr. Truelove!" he shouted. "You gotta come quick!"

"Ev, what is it?" Truelove asked, recognizing that this apparition was actually Ev Butrum.

"The ranch has been hit! Pete, Troy, an' Shorty have been shot dead!"

"What?" several men gasped.

"And the ranch has been set afire."

"Ev's right, Mr. Truelove, I can see the fire from here," one of the others called back into the house from the front porch.

Truelove and the others ran out onto the front porch. They could see the distant flames licking up into the night sky.

For a moment, everyone just stood there, mesmerized by the scene. Then, Vogel called them into action. "Well, come on!" he shouted. "If we get over there in time, we might be able to save some of it!"

"I've got extra buckets in the barn!" Baker said. "Get 'em in the wagons men, an' let's go!"

"What's the point?" Harley asked. "By the time we get there, it'll be too late."

"You're not going with us?" Doc Claymore asked his son.

"There's enough of you. You don't need me," Harley said. He took a bottle of whiskey from the sideboard, and tucked it under his arm. "I reckon I'll just get on back and keep an eye on our place. You never can tell where they might hit next."

Chapter 8

IT WAS QUIET WHERE WIN AND JOE WAITED IN THE ROCKS. They could hear crickets and frogs, a distant coyote and a closer owl, but nothing else. They strained their ears in vain for the muffled sounds of approaching men, the drum of horses' hooves, the rattle of the saddle and tack.

"Maybe they won't come this way," Win suggested.

"They'll come this way," Joe insisted. "It's the only way they can come, without running into the others."

"Shh, wait! There they are!" Win whispered. He had just gotten a glimpse of five men, silhouetted against the orange glow of the burning ranch. For a moment it was as if the gates of hell had opened, allowing five of its most desperate tenants to escape.

Win pulled his pistol and checked his load. Joe did the same.

The riders continued their ghostly approach, men and animals moving as softly and quietly as drifting smoke. Win cocked his pistol and raised it.

"Hold it right there!" he called.

"What the hell?" one of the men shouted. "Who is it?"

"Shoot 'im down!" another called.

The riders pulled their pistols then and opened fire. The night was brightly lit with the muzzle flashes and streaks of flame as Win, Joe, and the five mounted men exchanged gunfire. One of the men dropped from his saddle and skidded across hard ground. Flashes of orange light exploded like fire-balls on the rocks.

Win and Joe were well positioned in the rocks to pick out their targets. The outlaws, on the other hand, were astride horses that were rearing and twisting about nervously as flying lead whistled through the air and whined off stone.

Joe picked out one of the riders and tumbled him from the saddle.

"Where the hell are they?" one of the two remaining outlaws shouted in panic.

"Let's get out of here!" the other yelled.

They didn't make it.

Then it was quiet, with the final round of shooting but faint echoes bounding off distant hills. A little cloud of acrid-bitter gunsmoke drifted up over the deadly battlefield and Win and Joe walked out among the fallen rustlers, moving cautiously, their pistols at the ready.

It wasn't necessary. All five men were dead, and the entire battle had taken less than a minute.

Half a mile back down the trail, Clete Rawlings saw and heard the battle. His horse had picked up a rock and that delay caused him to fall behind the others. It also saved his life.

In the east, the sun was a full disk above the horizon. A dozen wagons were parked in the soft morning light, and in the wagons, nestled among the quilts and blankets, slept the children of the families who had come to help fight the fire. The morning light now disclosed the damage done. The main house and bunkhouse had been completely destroyed, but it could have been worse. Had Truelove not taken his wife and daughter with him to the meeting, they might now be lying dead in the smoldering ruins. The smoke house, granary, and barn had not burned because they were protected from the flames by the prodigious efforts of those who had come to fight the fire.

Martha Truelove stood in her husband's arms, weeping softly. Lucy stood close to her parents, looking at the destruction with eyes that were wide and sad. The Trueloves, like everyone else out there, were covered with ash and soot from the blackened ruins of their home. On the ground under a tree, sat a pitiful pile of what few belongings they had managed to pull from the ashes. Most of their belongings were burned and twisted beyond recognition, but here and there a few things had survived the flames and their bright, undamaged colors shined incongruously from the pile of smoking, blackened rubble. The cast-iron cook stove stood undamaged, almost defiantly, in the midst of what had been the kitchen.

Everyone was tired and filled with a great sadness for the three young cowboys who had been killed. In addition to their deaths, the death of a home was also particularly hard, because this was an area where homes and people were few and far between.

"How many were there?" Shelby asked Ev. This was the first chance he had had for interrogation, because the entire night had been passed in the effort to protect the other buildings.

"I'm not sure," Ev replied. "Four, five, six. I was too busy dodging bullets to count."

"Did you recognize any of them?"

Ev, who had helped fight the fire, was black with soot and ash. He walked over to the well and brought up a bucket of water, then took a long drink from the dipper, not yet having answered the marshal's question. He wiped the back of his hand across his mouth, leaving a clean swipe through the soot.

"Well?" Shelby asked again, impatient with Ev's stalling.

"I'm not real sure," Ev finally said. "Like I said, I was busy dodging bullets. And besides that, it was dark. But when they set fire to the main house, it lit up the yard some, and that's when I got a pretty good look at one of them. I wouldn't swear to it, you understand, but I'm pretty sure I recognized a couple of 'em."

"Who were they?" Claymore asked, coming over to join the conversation and showing, by his question, that he was as eager as the marshal to find the guilty party.

"Clete Rawlings was one of 'em."

"Clete Rawlings. It figures," Shelby said. "He's one of Potter's men, all right."

"The thing is, I'm sure I saw Johnny Simmons with 'em too."

"Johnny Simmons? Are you sure?" Shelby asked, his face plainly showing that the information was difficult for him to accept.

"Well, like I said, I don't know if I could swear to it," Ev hedged. "But it sure looked like him."

Shelby looked over at Doc Claymore. "Simmons works for you, don't he, Claymore?"

"He did work for me," Doc Claymore agreed. "But he doesn't anymore. He took his pay and rode on about a month ago. I'd be surprised if he fell in with Potter, though. I'm sure you're mistaken, Ev."

"I could be," Ev admitted. "But it sure looked like him."

"There's someone comin' in!" Baker called, and the men who had fought the fire all night long now stirred themselves to meet the riders.

"There's two of 'em, leadin' a string of horses," one of the others said. "What is it, a pack train?"

"No, look. Look what's on the horses. It's bodies."

There were gasps of shock and surprise from all present, and they hurried out to meet the riders as they approached.

"It's the Coulters," Vogel said.

As Win and Joe rode into the front yard of what had been Truelove's house, they saw the men and women gathering together to meet them. Win signaled Joe, then they stopped near one of the wagons. Win climbed down from his horse and, taking his canteen from the pommel, walked over to the well to fill it. All eyes were on him, not only the men, but the women and children as well. The men crowded down close, the women hung back, and the children were back, farther, in some cases hiding behind their mothers' skirts, peering out around them with wide, curious, and in some cases, frightened, eyes.

"Coulter, you want to tell us what all this is about?" Doc Claymore asked.

As Win poured water into his canteen he looked around at the smoking ruins of what had been the house.

"Doesn't seem like you should have to ask," he said.

"See here, Coulter, are you saying these men did this?" Shelby asked.

"That's what I'm saying."

"How do you know they did it?" Baker asked.

Win put the top on his canteen and hooked it over the pommel.

"There's five of them. I believe our deal was, two-hundred fifty dollars each," Win said.

"You haven't answered my question, Coulter," Baker said. "How do you know these are the men who did it, unless you saw them do it? And if you saw them, why didn't you stop them then?"

Shelby had walked over to the six horses and was checking each of the men by grabbing a handful of hair and lifting the head.

"I'll be damned, Ev. You were right. This one is Johnny Simmons," he said.

Ev went over to Simmons's body and grabbed a handful of hair. He lifted the head and stared into the face. Simmons's eyes were open, but they were opaque with a death stare. Ev looked up at Joe, who was still sitting quietly on his horse. "I just wish it had been me instead of one of you that shot 'em. They killed Shorty, Curly, and Troy."

"It doesn't really matter who killed him, does it?" Joe asked. "He's just as dead."

"Yeah," Ev said. He let the head fall back down, then brushed his hands together. "Yeah, I reckon the son of a bitch is, at that."

"All right, boys, if you two will come into town tomorrow, I'll have a bank draft for twelve hundred fifty dollars drawn in your favor," Claymore offered.

Win nodded, then remounted his horse. "We'll see you tomorrow," he said. Touching his hat as if in greeting to the ladies, he and Joe rode away from the Truelove Ranch, leaving behind the gruesome cargo they had brought in.

It was late that afternoon when Clete Rawlings approached the entrance to a canyon that was about ten miles northwest of the Truelove Ranch. The canyon was known as Hidden Canyon, for the simple reason that it was so well concealed by the rocks and ridge lines which guarded its entrance that it couldn't be

seen unless someone was specifically looking for it. At the
entrance to the canyon there were two tall natural obelisks
from which someone could keep a watchful eye, thus pre-
venting anyone from approaching the canyon without being
seen. Down inside the canyon there was a source of water.

For these virtues Emil Potter had selected Hidden Canyon
as his hideout. There were half a dozen adobe shacks to house
the rustlers, as well as the handful of women, most of whom
were burned-out soiled doves, who had joined the group.

As Rawlings approached the canyon entrance, he stopped
and removed his hat, then waved it broadly across the top of
his head, put it back on, then took it off and waved it a second
time. This was the prescribed signal, and only then did he see
the series of mirror flashes which told him he could enter.

Potter was told that a rider was coming in, so he came
outside his cabin to wait. Potter, a short but powerfully built
man, suffered from some rare affliction that made him almost
completely hairless; he was not only bald, but lacked eyebrows
and beard as well. As a result, his head looked somewhat like
a cannonball. He had been eating when he heard that someone
was coming, so he wrapped a tortilla around some beans and
took it outside with him. Some of the juice dribbled down his
chin but he made no effort to wipe it off.

"It's Rawlings," someone said.

"Rawlings? Alone?"

"Yeah."

"I wonder what happened to the others?"

The rustlers and the women who had made the canyon their
home knew that six riders had gone out yesterday. They were
curious as to why only one was returning, and they drew close
to see what Rawlings would have to say. The women of the
camp hung back, out of the way of the men, but still close
enough to hear the news. One of the women was an olive-
skinned, black-eyed señorita named Rosa. Though no one but
her closest friend knew it, she was carrying Johnny Simmons's
child. She hadn't even told Johnny yet, because she was afraid
he would leave if he knew.

"What happened?" Potter asked.

"You ain't goin' to like it," Rawlings said.

"Tell me anyway."

"It's about the Coulter brothers," Rawlings said. "You know that the Cattlemen's Association hired them."

"Yeah, I heard about 'em."

"Well, they was waitin' for us. They threw down on us from the rocks, had three killed 'fore we even knew we was in danger. I managed to fight my way out," Rawlings lied, "but none of the others was that lucky. The Coulters killed 'em all."

"Johnny's dead?" Rosa asked with a gasp.

"Johnny Simmons? Yeah, he was the first one to be killed," Rawlings said coldly.

"Oh, Johnny!" Rosa wailed, and she wandered away crying, comforted by one of the others.

"What about Truelove's ranch?" Potter asked. "Did you get the job done?"

Potter smiled. "Yeah. We killed all his hands, and burned his house and bunkhouse," Potter said, smiling proudly."

"Good job! Good job!" Potter said happily. He smiled in triumph. "With most all his hands dead, that mean's Truelove's cows are there for the takin'. I reckon we'll pay 'em a visit tonight."

It was late in the afternoon of the day after the fire. The neighbors who had gathered to fight the fire were all gone now. Only Truelove, his wife and daughter, and Ev remained behind to see to the cleanup. A wagon, its wood bleached white by the sun, sat a few feet in front of the blackened remains of the house, as it was being filled with the ashes and burned boards to be hauled away. All four were working when Lucy saw two riders approaching.

"Pa, Ma, here comes two men," she called to the others.

"Who is it?" Truelove asked.

Looking up, Ev shielded his eyes against the sun. "It's the Coulters, Mr. Truelove," he said.

"I wonder what they want?" Martha said. "They frighten me."

"You've got no reason to be frightened of them," Truelove said.

"I know. You've told me the story of how they saved your life during the war. And I know they're on our side. But I've heard so much about them. They are violent men," Martha said, with a shudder.

"It is a violent world," Truelove replied. "Sometimes you need a little violence on your side." He started toward the riders. "Howdy, Win, Joe. What can I do for you boys?" he asked.

Both Win and Joe dismounted. Win handed the reins of his horse to Joe, who then led both animals over to the watering trough to let them drink.

"Mr. Truelove, how many head of cattle do you have?" Win asked.

"About twenty-five hundred or so," Truelove answered. "Why do you ask?"

"Because, unless I miss my guess, Emil Potter will be coming after them soon."

"By soon, you mean when?"

"Tonight."

"Oh," Martha gasped.

Truelove patted his wife's hand reassuringly, then looked at Ev.

"Ev, I figure you got wages comin'," he said. "I'm goin' to pay you off now so you can get out of here."

"Are you firin' me, Mr. Truelove?" Ev asked.

"No, not exactly. You can come back tomorrow . . . if I have any cows left. You'll still have your job if you want it. But I don't figure this is your fight, so I want you to take Martha and Lucy on into town."

"What do you mean, take me into town?" Martha asked. "I'm staying out here. You can't fight them off by yourself," she protested.

"He won't be by himself, Mrs. Truelove," Win said. "My brother and I will be here with him."

"You? Why would you do such a thing?" Truelove asked. "It isn't your fight."

"Oh but it is. The Cattlemen's Association is paying us to make it our fight, remember? We'll be right here when they come."

"I will too," Ev said.

"Ev, you sure you want to do this?" Truelove asked.

"I'm sure. I figure I owe 'em for Troy, Shorty and Curly," Ev said. "Besides that, I put too much work in these cows just to see someone ride in and take 'em away."

Truelove smiled. "Well, that's the mark of a good foreman, I reckon."

"Foreman?" Ev smiled broadly. "Look here, Mr. Truelove, are you tellin' me you're makin' me the foreman of this ranch?"

Truelove laughed. "I reckon I am," he said. "Seeing as how you're the only hand I got left. But if we don't keep Potter from takin' all our cows tonight, there won't be no ranch to be foreman of."

"We'll stop him, Mr. Truelove," Ev said. "You just tell me what you want me to do."

Truelove looked at Win and Joe. "Well, I reckon that's up to these boys. Have either of you got any ideas?"

"Yeah, a few," Win admitted

"Can they wait until after we've had a meal?" Martha asked. "It's gettin' on toward suppertime. I thought I'd fix us somethin' to eat."

"Thank you, but we've got some jerky in our saddle bags," Win said.

Joe got a pained expression on his face. "Hold it, what are you doing turning down a meal?" he asked.

Win pointed to the burned-out house. "I figure these folks got enough to deal with, without having to worry about cooking a meal."

"Nonsense," Martha said. "The rest of us have to eat, don't we? What's two more mouths to feed? Anyway, the stove is still here and I've just about got it cleaned up and ready to use. And the smokehouse is still full of meat. If we're going to fight a war tonight, we're goin' to do it on a full stomach."

"Mrs. Truelove, you are a lady after my own heart," Joe said. He looked at Win, pleadingly. "What do you say, Win?"

Win smiled, and nodded. "All right," he said. "I guess there's no arguing with you when you're hungry." He looked at Martha. "If you are certain it won't put you out any."

Martha laughed. "Mr. Coulter . . . the house has been burned down around us. Would you please tell me how in the Sam Hill I could be put out anymore than I already am? Come on, Lucy. Help me feed these hungry men."

Chapter 9

JOE FOUND A PLACE UNDER A TREE. WIN WAS SITTING ON AN overturned bucket, eating a supper of pork chops, fried potatoes and scrambled eggs. Truelove, who had just finished his own supper, came over to talk to him.

"You been givin' some thought to what we might do tonight?" he asked. "I mean, do you have any ideas on how we can stop Potter?"

"I've been givin' it some thought," Win said. He put down his plate, then stood up and pointed to the open end of the valley. "Anyone who comes in is going to have to come that way, unless they come over the mountains."

"That's right," Truelove agreed. He chuckled. "And even if they could get in that way, they couldn't get nothin' back out unless they was stealin' mountain goats."

"All we need to do is pick us out a few good places and wait. Once they come in, we'll open up on them. Only thing is . . . we should get into place before it gets dark so we all know where everyone else is. That way we'll know not to shoot each other."

"Win, suppose we light a lantern and hang it in the granary?" Joe suggested.

"Why would you want to do that?" Truelove asked. "Seems to me like that would just draw 'em in."

Win and Joe looked at Truelove and smiled. Then, Truelove

nodded. "I see what you mean," he said. "We'll be usin' the lantern as bait."

"I'll hang the lantern," Martha offered.

"Good," Win answered. He pointed to the barn. "I'll be up in the loft with a rifle. Joe?"

"Yeah?"

"You think you can get up onto the smokehouse without eating everything that's in it?"

Joe laughed. "I reckon I could, if I took a pork chop or two to gnaw on," he teased.

"Mr. Truelove, you and Ev set up behind these two water troughs," Win said. "The water will help stop the bullets."

"Till it all leaks out," Truelove said with a chuckle.

"Well, if we haven't run 'em off by the time all the water can leak through a couple of bullet holes, we'll prob'ly be dead, anyway," Ev suggested.

"Oh!" Martha gasped.

Realizing what he had said, Ev apologized quickly. "Miz Truelove, don't pay no attention to that," Ev said. "I was just funnin', that's all."

"You have a most unusual sense of humor, Mr. Butrum," Martha said.

"Yes'm, I reckon I do. I apologize about that."

"No apology needed, Mr. Butrum."

"What about me?" Lucy asked Win. "Where do you want me to go?"

"I want you and your mother to get down into the root cellar and stay there," Win ordered.

"What do you mean? You aren't keeping me out of this," Lucy complained.

"Lucy, do what Mr. Coulter says."

"But Pa, you know I can shoot as well as most men."

"I know you can, honey, when you're shooting at tin cans, or bottles and the like," Truelove said. "But this is for real, and I don't aim to take any chances with you or your mother."

Lucy pouted, but said nothing else.

"Well," Win said, walking over to his horse and pulling a rifle out of the saddle holster. He took a box of shells from the saddlebag. "I guess we'd better get to it while it's still light."

Everyone started moving into their own positions. Lucy, who was still pouting, didn't move.

"Lucy, go on now," Truelove scolded gently.

With one more defiant look, Lucy turned and walked toward her mother, who was now washing the dishes in a bucket of water.

With his rifle in hand, Win climbed up into the hayloft over the barn, then started looking toward the west, toward the open end of the draw, from which direction Potter and his men would be coming.

From this vantage point, Win could see why Truelove had chosen this particular setting to build his house. He was treated to one of the vistas he had come to greatly appreciate during his years of wandering through the West. The setting sun, losing both heat and brilliance, but none of its vibrant orange color, seemed poised in the west above the desert floor. A dark gray haze was beginning to gather in the notches of the rugged escarpment, hanging there like drifting smoke. The red sandy loam was dotted with blue cedar and mesquite, limned in gold from the setting sun.

"It's beautiful, isn't it?" a woman's voice said.

Startled, Win turned to see Lucy just coming off the ladder, onto the loft. She was carrying a rifle.

"What are you doing here?" Win asked harshly.

"This is my home, Mr. Coulter," Lucy said. "Or at least, what is left of it," she added. "I don't care what you or Pa say, I don't intend to sit on my hands while someone tries to take it away from us."

"This is no place for a woman," Win insisted.

Lucy held up her rifle. "The bullet that comes out of here doesn't know whether it's been shot by a man or a woman," she said. "I'm staying, and there is nothing you can do about it, unless you plan to throw me out of here physically."

Win stroked his chin for a moment as he stared at her. She was right, there wasn't anything he could do about it. And, if she had that much gumption, maybe she would be useful.

"All right," he agreed, reluctantly. "You can stay."

"Ha," Lucy said with a snort. "As if I needed your permission."

Despite himself, Win laughed.

Win looked around to find the others. He saw Joe lying on his stomach on top of the smokehouse. Ev was kneeling behind one of the watering troughs, peering intently over the top. Truelove was lying on his stomach, peering around the edge of the other watering trough.

"Looks like everyone is where they're supposed to be," Win said quietly. "Everyone except you." He turned toward her and saw that she had been staring at him.

"Mr. Coulter," she started.

"Call me Win."

"Win. Do you think I'm pretty?" Lucy asked.

Win chuckled.

"What is it? Why are you laughing?" Lucy asked sharply.

"Here we are, waiting for a shooting war to begin with who knows how many rustlers, and you want to know if I think you're pretty."

"Well, am I?"

Win looked at her. She was flirting openly with him now. Sometimes, innocent young women tended to do that. He never really knew whether they were attracted to him out of gratitude when he helped them, or out of a sense of excitement from the danger he represented to them. Whatever the reason, he didn't like to encourage it. He had a thousand reasons why such a thing shouldn't be encouraged, none of which he was willing to share because the very act of sharing why he couldn't be interested could, in itself, be mistakenly construed as an act of encouragement. If he needed a woman there was always Big Kate's Place, or a soiled dove in the next town. He neither needed, nor wanted, any involvement with some fresh-scrubbed rancher's daughter.

"Miss Truelove, when this is all over, I'll be drifting on," Win said quietly.

Lucy looked down at the toe of her boot. She knew he had read her mind and she knew he was telling her now that she was barking up the wrong tree. And yet, she couldn't bring herself to turn away from him. She had to try one more time to see if there was something, down inside the man, she could appeal to.

"You know, Win," she said, pawing at the ground self-consciously with her foot. "There's a lot of good grazing land in this valley, more than enough to support two or three families. If you were ever interested in, well, maybe in starting your own ranch, you could do worse than to do it here."

"I'm sure I could," Win said. He looked at her for a moment, then his voice softened. "Lucy, I can't settle down here. I can't settle down anywhere. If I did, I would get homesick."

Lucy was clearly confused. "Homesick? How could you be homesick? I thought you didn't live anywhere. I thought you were as loose as a tumbleweed."

Win chuckled. "I am," he said. "And that's what I would get homesick for. That's the worst kind of homesick you can have."

"I . . . I understand," Lucy said.

"I hope you do," Win said quietly. "You're as fine a young woman as I've ever run across, and you deserve a fine man. I'm not that man."

"I guess I made a fool out of myself," Lucy said. "I'm sorry."

Win smiled at her. "I expect in a few days I'll probably look back on this and figure I was the one made a fool of himself," he said. He looked out toward the gathering dusk. "Can you really shoot, Lucy Truelove?"

Lucy laughed. "I can snuff a candle at a hundred yards. Is that good enough shooting for you?"

"Good enough," Win agreed. He pointed over to the corner of the barn. "You get over there," he said. "The wall is double-planked there, and the vent-hole is big enough for you to poke your rifle through."

"Not much for picking out targets though," Lucy complained.

Despite himself, Win chuckled. "You'd complain if you were hung with a new rope," he said. "You're up here, aren't you? If I had my way, you'd be back in the root cellar. Now, get over there like I said."

Lucy smiled. "Yes, sir," she said. "Whatever you say, sir." She saluted.

Once Lucy got into position, Win stepped back up to the door and resumed his watch. It was dark and quiet. Over by the granary, the lantern burned brightly. A coyote howled and an owl hooted.

There was the scratch of hooves on the ground and the creak of riders in saddle leather. Emil Potter twisted in his saddle and stared down toward the ranch. The house and bunkhouse were gone, but there was a single lantern burning in one of the remaining outbuildings. It seemed incredible to him that they had managed to sneak up on Truelove's ranch without being seen, but that was just what had happened.

"Watch out!" someone said in a short, angry voice.

"Keep it quiet," Potter hissed. "You want them to hear us?"

"Hell, what if they do? Who's here? One man, his wife and daughter? Even the ranch hands is gone."

"Nevertheless, keep quiet," Potter said. "No sense in lettin' 'em know we're here."

"They're goin' to find out pretty soon," one of the men said. He laughed a short, evil laugh. "Especially the girl. I aim to make a special point to let her know I'm here."

"Only if you beat me to her," one of the others added, and they all laughed.

"I wouldn't be worryin' none about the girl," Potter said. "When I give the word, I want ever'one to shoot toward that lantern. Like as not they're all inside there, and, small as it is, if we shoot it up good we'll prob'ly get all of 'em. But, don't shoot until we get closer and I give the word.

"Right," one of his men agreed.

Win saw them coming, and, though it was now too dark to signal his brother, he knew that Joe had seen them too. He knew, also, that Joe knew enough not to shoot until they were close enough for the first shot to be effective.

"Win!" Lucy hissed. "They're comin'!"

"Yes, I know," Win called back, quietly. "Lucy, don't shoot until I shoot."

"All right," Lucy replied.

Win raised his rifle and waited. They were still too far away and it was too dark to make them out well enough for a shot, or even to determine exactly how many there were. Then, finally, they drew close enough. He saw them raise their rifles and aim at the lantern in the granary. Joe's trick was working.

"Fire!" one of the riders barked.

With the muzzle flash from their rifles, Win had a target. He squeezed off a round, firing just to the right and slightly below one of the muzzle flashes. He heard a grunt of pain.

"What the hell? Where did that come from?"

Win's firing was a signal for the others to open fire as well, and Joe, Truelove, and Ev began shooting.

"What the hell? They been waitin' for us with a whole army!" one of the attackers shouted in a frightened voice. "We got to get the hell out of here!"

Win heard the sound of hoofbeats as the night-riders turned their horses and began beating a retreat. The defenders fired three or four more times but they were just shooting in the dark with no idea as to where their targets were. It didn't really matter. The idea now was simply to run them off, and that they did.

Win shouted down to the others. "All right! Hold your fire! Save your ammunition! They're gone!"

Win and Lucy climbed down from the hayloft, then joined Joe, who jumped down from the top of the smokehouse.

"Anyone get hit?" Win asked.

"No, but I think we hit a few of those bastards!" Ev said, still excited, flushed with victory over their successful skirmish.

"We did it!" Truelove said. "By golly, we ran them off! They won't be back!"

"Not tonight," Win agreed. "And maybe not to your ranch at all, but most of 'em got away and if they don't come here, they'll try somewhere else."

"There's at least three of 'em won't try anywhere else," Joe said somberly.

"Three of them," Win said. "Those three are yours, Mr. Truelove. At two hundred fifty dollars each, that's seven hundred and fifty dollars. You think you could rebuild your ranch house with seven hundred and fifty dollars?"

"Oh, no, I couldn't," Truelove said.

"Sure you can," Joe said, seconding his brother's offer.

"I just wouldn't feel right trafficking in another man's death," Truelove said.

"Otis Truelove, don't be a fool," Martha said determinedly, coming out of the root cellar then, to join them. "You and Ev and Lucy helped kill those men."

"Lucy? What do you mean, Lucy helped?"

"She ran out of the root cellar before it all started," Martha said. "I thought she came to join you."

"No, I didn't know anything about it," Truelove said.

"I was in the barn, Pa. With Mr. Coulter."

Truelove looked at Win. "I hope she didn't get in your way," he said.

"Not at all. She handled herself very well," Win said.

"But about your offer . . ."

"Otis, if these men are generous enough to make this offer, I don't intend to let you refuse. If you won't take the bodies into town and claim the reward for them, I will."

Truelove sighed, then looked at Win and Joe. "I thank you boys," he said.

Win nodded, then looked over at Joe. "I reckon we'd better be going," he said.

"Where are you going?" Lucy asked.

"Out there," Win answered without elaboration.

"But, where will you be if we need you? If this happens again?"

"We'll be around," Joe replied.

Chapter 10

IN LESS THAN TWO DAYS THE VALLEY HAD BEEN TURNED INTO a battlefield. The Cattlemen's Association had now paid bounty on eight rustlers. Rustlers or not, the sudden demise of eight young men quickly became the subject of every conversation in every bar in town.

"The Coulters got them first five, you'll remember, then when that bunch hit Truelove's place why, he and Ev got three more," one man explained.

"I heard that the Coulters got them, too, but they just give them to Truelove to give him enough money to rebuild his house."

Harley Claymore listened to the babble of conversation. He was a listener, rather than participant, because even though conversations were going on all around him, he wasn't included. It wasn't an effort in concert by the others to exclude him. It was just that Harley was known as an arrogant young man with a quick temper. The best way to avoid any trouble with him, was to avoid, as much as possible, any contact with him.

Thus it was that, while social discourse went on at a fevered pitch all about him, Harley sat at a table with Angus Spahn and Deekus Cain. Harley was playing a game of Ole' Sol, though he would have preferred a game of poker. Unfortunately, neither Spahn nor Cain had enough money to play cards, and no one else would play with him, because they didn't want to risk to getting him angry.

Harley was not someone a person wanted to get angry. He was very good with his guns, and most believed that he looked, openly, for opportunities to use them. Last year, over in Sulphur Springs, he killed a man in a poker game after the man accused him of cheating. Of course Harley had been cheating, but he couldn't let the accusation go unchallenged. The other man drew first, so there were no charges filed against Harley, even though he had goaded the other man into drawing.

The story was that Harley had also killed a man over in Loganville for somewhat the same reason, but no one was really sure about that. That was because Harley hadn't given that man a chance to draw. Instead, he had waited outside the saloon, and when the man came out some time later, Harley shot him down from ambush. Though neither of the two men Harley had killed were known to be gunfighters they were, nevertheless, victims, and victims were all he needed to enhance his reputation as a man to be avoided.

Harley counted out three cards but couldn't find a play. The second card of the three was a black seven. There would have been a play had it come up on top. Unfortunately, it was one card down and therefore useless to him. Harley glared at it for a moment, then, with a shrug, played it anyway.

The bat-wing doors swung open and a cowboy came in and walked over to the bar. He was a working cowhand, not a gunman, and Harely recognized him as someone who rode for Vogel, though Harley didn't know the cowboy's name. The cowboy ordered a whiskey, then looked around and saw Harley sitting at the table, calmly playing cards.

"I just been thinkin' about Pete, Troy, and Shorty," the cowboy said to no one in particular. "They was good hands, cowmen who never did no harm to nobody. And they was shot down in cold blood."

Though the cowboy wasn't telling the people in the saloon anything they didn't already know, no one responded to his outburst. He had obviously been drinking before he came here and now he was in an expansive and dangerous mood.

"They was shot down in cold blood and the Truelove Ranch, where they worked, was burned out," the cowboy went on. "But then, you was all out there helpin' to fight the fire . . . you all seen it," he said. He looked around the room, then his eyes fell on Harley who was still, pointedly, dealing and studying his cards. "That is, ever'one who was out there helpin' put out the fire seen it.

"But you wasn't there, was you, Harley Claymore? You and them two egg-sucking mongrels you got hanging around you all the time," he added with a derisive slur toward Spahn and Cain. "Tell us how is it that you three wasn't out there to help fight the fire at the Truelove Ranch, like the rest of us."

Harley looked up nonchalantly. "You talkin' to me, cowboy?"

"Am I talkin' to you?" the cowboy repeated. "Hell yes I'm talkin' to you, you low-assed, card-cheatin' son of a bitch."

The others in the saloon gasped at the cowboy's careless choice of words. Harley, however, just smiled coldly.

"Hey, do you know who you're talkin' to?" Spahn started, but Harely put his hand out to quiet him.

"It's all right, Angus," he said. "The cowboy is just drunk, that's all. I'm inclined to let that remark pass."

"You're a lucky man," Spahn said. "Harley wouldn't let somethin' like that pass with most men."

"I don't want him to let it pass. I asked how come it is, that you three wasn't out to help fight the fire at the Truelove Ranch with the rest of us?"

"Why should I be out there?" Harely replied. "I've got my own ranch to run." He rifled through the cards as he talked, and found another play on the table.

"What do you mean, you've got a ranch to run? You got nothin' to say 'bout what goes on out at the Claymore spread. Hell, ever'body knows you don't even take a piss, 'lessen your pa tells you you can."

Harley looked up from the cards again. This time the nonchalance was gone. Instead, his eyes were narrowed menacingly. "Cowboy, I don't believe I know your name," he said.

"My name is Peabody. Earl Peabody. Not that it makes any difference to you."

"Oh, that's where you're wrong. It does make a difference to me, Peabody. You see, me an' you are about to have us a fight."

Peabody grinned broadly. "A fight? Yeah," he said. "That would be jake by me. Let's see, there's three of you and one of me, but I don't figure those two pissants you have with you got enough gumption to join in." Peabody made his hands into fists then held them out in front of his face, moving his right hand in tiny circles. "Come on," he said. "I'm goin' to enjoy this."

"I'm afraid not, Mr. Peabody," Harley said. "That isn't the kind of fight I'm talkin' about. I plan to make this permanent."

Peabody lowered his fists slightly, staring at Harley with a confused expression on his face. "What do you mean, make it permanent?"

"We'll fight with guns, not with fists."

Peabody croaked what might have been laughter. "Yeah, you yellow-bellied bastard. I figured you might want to try something like that. That's why I ain't carryin' no gun with me. No, sir. We're goin' to settle this like men. We won't be using guns."

"Oh, but we will," Harley said. "Everyone in here heard you challenge me."

"No, they heard me call you a low-assed, card-cheatin' son of a bitch," Peabody said, grinning broadly. He still wasn't aware of the extent of his danger. "You the one that challenged me." He began making tiny circles with his right fist. "So, come on, let's get on with it."

"Yes, let's do," Harley said. He stood up and stepped away from the table, letting his arm hang down alongside his pistol as he looked at the cowboy through cold, ruthless eyes. "I'll let you draw first."

"I told you, I ain't drawin' on you," Peabody repeated. "No, come on over here and take your beatin' like a man."

"I said draw," Harley repeated in a cold, flat voice.

The others in the saloon knew, well before Peabody, that the cowboy had carried things too far. There was going to be gunplay and they began, quietly but deliberately, to get out of the way of any flying lead.

It wasn't until that moment, seeing the others move out of the way, that Peabody began to worry that he might actually be losing control of the situation. He was still holding his fists in front of him, and he lowered them, then stared at Harley incredulously. "Are you deaf, Claymore? Ain't you been hearin' me tell you that I'm not wearin' a gun? If you're fi-gurin' on forcin' me into a fight, you can just figure again, 'cause I ain't goin' to do it."

"I'll give you time to get yourself heeled," Harley offered.

"I told you, I ain't goin' to get into no gunfight with you."

"If you aren't goin' to fight, then get out of here. Get out of this saloon, out of this town, and out of this valley. Leave with your tail tucked between your legs, like the cowardly mongrel you are."

"No, I ain't doin' that, either," Peabody said. "I got a right to live where I want and to say what I want." He picked up his drink, hoping by that action to show his defiance. What he showed instead was his fear, for his hand was shaking so badly that some of the whiskey sloshed over.

"You got no rights that I don't let you have," Harley growled. "Now, you walk through that door right now, or pull a gun."

"I told you, I'm not packin' a gun."

"Somebody give him one," Harley said coldly. He pulled his lips into a sinister smile. "Mr. Peabody seems to have come to this fight unprepared."

"I don't want a gun," Peabody said.

When no one offered Peabody their gun, Harley pointed to another cowboy who was standing at the far end of the bar. This man was carrying a pistol.

"Give him your gun," Harley ordered. "You aren't going to be using it."

"He don't want a gun," the man said.

"Oh, I think he does."

"Listen, Harley, you don't want to pay Peabody any mind. He was good friends with them boys that was killed out at

Truelove's place and he's just upset, that's all. Why don't you just leave it be?''

"I said give him your gun."

"I ain't goin' to do that. If I give him a gun, you'll kill him."

"That's right."

"Well, then I don't want no part of it."

"You have no choice, my friend. You'll either give him your gun so I can kill him, or keep it for yourself, and I'll kill you," Harley said. He turned three-quarters of the way toward the armed cowboy. "Which will it be?"

"Now, hold it! This ain't my fight!" the cowboy said, holding out his hands, as if by that action he could stop Harley from doing anything.

"Give him your gun, or use it yourself," Harley said again.

The cowboy paused for just a moment longer, then sighed in defeat. "All right, all right. If you put it that way, I reckon I'll do whatever you want." He took his gun out of the holster and lay it on the bar. "Sorry, Peabody," he said. He gave the gun a shove and it slid half-way down the bar, smashing through two glasses, then stopping just beside Peabody's hand. It rocked back and forth for a moment, making a little sound that, in the now-silent bar, seemed almost deafening.

"Pick it up," Harley said to Peabody.

Peabody looked at the pistol. A vein was jumping in his neck, and those who were close enough to him could see his hands shaking.

"Do it," Harley said again.

"No, I ain't goin' to. No matter what you do, you can't make me fight."

"I'm counting to three," Harley said. "When I get to three, you had better reach for that gun because I'm going to pull mine."

"No, I told you!"

"One," Harley said coldly.

"I said no!"

"Two."

Suddenly Peabody made a desperate claw for the pistol. Harley smiled, because this was exactly what he had wanted

Peabody to do. It was obvious, now, that it was a fair fight. He had told the cowboy he would count to three and, here Peabody was, cheating, trying to draw the gun before three.

Because the pistol was lying on the bar and not in a holster at his side, Peabody was at a distinct disadvantage. The gun would be much more difficult to pick up, than it would have been to draw.

"Three," Harley said, finishing the count, even as Peabody was making a desperate grab for the pistol.

Harley pulled his own gun then. He held it for a second, then looked around at all the others in the bar as if emphasizing that he was being more than fair. Then, just as Peabody brought the gun around, Harley fired. His bullet caught Peabody in the neck and Peabody dropped his gun, unfired, and clutched his throat. He fell back against the bar, then slid down, dead before he reached the floor.

Harley looked around the saloon, a broad smile on his face. "Well, so much for the loud-mouthed Mr. Peabody," he said. "Anyone else have anything to say?"

Everyone studied their glass or bottle, avoiding Harley's eyes.

"Harley Claymore kilt 'im fair and square, and you all seen it," Spahn shouted. "Anyone plannin' on sayin' it was anything other than a fair fight?"

"I seen it too," Cain added. "The cowboy went for the gun first. Fact is, he cheated. He started reachin' for it before Harley counted to three."

The sound of the gunshot brought two or three outsiders into the saloon, including Marshal Shelby. Shelby saw Peabody sitting down against the bar, his eyes open and sightless, his hand clenched tightly around the unfired pistol. Then he saw Harley standing in the middle of the saloon floor, looking smug and defiant.

"Oh, hell," Shelby said quietly. "I might have known you would have something to do with this."

"Look in Peabody's hand, Marshal," Spahn said. "If Harley hadn't shot him, he would've shot Harley."

"Is that the way it was?" Shelby asked the others. When

no one answered, Shelby asked the bartender directly. "Fred, is he calling it right?"

"You heard what Spahn and Cain said," Fred replied.

"You know them two. Harley could say the sun set in the east, and Spahn and Cain would swear to it. Now I'm asking you. How did it happen?"

"Peabody ain't got nobody to blame but his ownself," Fred said. "He come in here lookin' for trouble."

"Then you're backin' up Harley? You are saying he killed Peabody in self-defense?"

Fred looked at the others in the bar but, as before, none of them would return his gaze. No one seemed willing to comment.

"I guess you could call it self-defense," Fred said. "Peabody was tryin' to throw down on him, but it would'a taken him till next Sunday to do it."

"But, it was self-defense?" Shelby asked.

Fred sighed. "Yeah, it was self-defense."

Shelby looked at Harley. "One of these days, Harley, you're goin' to run up against someone who ain't a pushover. When you do, I'll be takin' your body over to the undertaker's, then ridin' out to tell your pa."

"I wouldn't be worryin' 'bout anything like that happening," Harley said.

"Oh, it'll happen," Shelby said. "I don't know when, or where, but it'll happen." He looked toward a couple of Rocking V hands. "He belongs to you boys," he said. "Take him over to the undertaker. I'll come along to make the arrangements."

The two cowboys picked up their fallen friend and carried him out the door, followed by the marshal.

"Ha!" Harley said after the marshal left. "Shelby thinks there might be someone around who can put me on the floor. Anyone got any idea who that might be?" He whipped his gun out and spun the cylinder. "Anybody in here want to try that little deed?" He waved the gun around the room and as it passed, the men either ducked or averted their eyes. Harley laughed again, then he put the gun away. "I didn't think so."

"You the fastest there is, Harley. They ain't nobody goin' to tangle with you," Spahn said.

"Yeah, nobody," Cain added. "You're too good."

Excitedly, Harley tossed down the rest of his whiskey, then he stood up. "I'm goin' down to Big Kate's Place," he said. "I need me a woman."

"What about us?" Spahn asked.

"What about you? You got money enough for a woman?"

Spahn and Cain looked at each other sheepishly. They had hoped, by their hinting, to be included in the trip to Big Kate's. But that would have taken an advance from Harley, and he made no such offer.

"No," Spahn finally said. "We ain't got no money."

"You want us to wait here for you? We'll wait here if you want us to," Cain said, when it became obvious that Harley wasn't going to give them any money.

"Yeah, Harley, you know us. We'll do whatever you ask us to do," Spahn added.

"You two go on back out to the ranch. I'll see you later."

"Yeah," Cain said. "Me and Spahn will go on out to the ranch."

"We'll see you later," Spahn called to Harley as he left the saloon.

Harley rode down to the end of the street, then tied his horse in front of Big Kate's Place. Big Kate met him in the front room.

"What do want, Harley?" she asked.

"What do I want? What do you mean, what do I want? What does anyone want when they come to a whore house?" Harley replied.

"I've already heard about what happened down at the saloon a while ago. I don't want any trouble like that in here."

Harley smiled. "You heard already, huh? Boy, news really travels fast." Looking around the salon, he saw Kelly Milhall over by the piano, trying to make herself inconspicuous. "Kelly," he said, pointing. "I want Kelly. Tell her to come here."

Big Kate shook her head. "I don't tell any of my girls who they have to go with," she said. "It's up to them."

"Yeah?" Harley said. "Well, Kelly's going to want to come with me, ain't you, girly?"

Hiding her fear behind a practiced smile, Kelly nodded in the affirmative, then led Harley toward the stairs.

Chapter 11

IT HAD BEEN FIFTEEN MINUTES SINCE HARLEY CLAYMORE took Kelly upstairs with him, and Big Kate glanced up nervously. None of her girls had ever made any specific complaints about being with Harley, but she had noticed that none of them ever seemed anxious to be with him.

That in itself was a cause for curiosity, if not worry. Harley was the son of a very wealthy man, and Big Kate knew that it was the fantasy of many girls who were on the line to meet a wealthy man who could take them away from "the life." Harley seemed like an ideal candidate for such a fantasy, and yet every time he came around the girls tried to avoid him.

"What does a fella have to do to get a beer around this place?"

Looking up, Big Kate saw Joe Coulter. She smiled broadly at the bigger of the two brothers who had become very popular with the girls since taking rooms here.

"All you have to do is ask," Big Kate said.

"I'm asking," Joe said. "I've got that much dust in my craw that General Pemberton could have used it to build enough redoubts to hold out the entire Yankee Army."

Laughing, Big Kate drew a mug of beer and handed it to him.

"Is Kelly around?" Joe asked.

"Busy," Big Kate answered, without elaboration. "Sorry."

"That's all right, she has to make a living just like everyone else."

"You boys haven't been staying in your rooms much, lately," Big Kate said. "You aren't giving them up, are you?"

"No," Joe answered. "We've been keeping busy, but it's nice knowing they're here when we can get around to them."

"Were you down at the saloon for all the excitement earlier?" Big Kate asked.

"What excitement?" Joe asked as he took another swallow of his beer.

"A cowboy named Peabody got himself shot."

Joe wiped the foam from his lips with the back of his hand. "Murder? Or fair fight?"

"They're calling it a fair fight, but from what I hear, there wasn't much fair about it. Harley Claymore goaded the cowboy into it."

"I've known a lot of men like Harley Claymore," Joe said. "They usually end up goading the wrong person into a fight, but not until they've killed their share of poor dumb bastards who didn't have enough sense to stay away from them."

Kelly came down the stairs and went over to the bar, where she picked up a bottle and two glasses. Seeing her, Joe smiled and started toward her. "Hi, Kelly," he said.

"I'm . . . I'm busy, Joe," Kelly replied, turning away from him as he approached her. "I just came down to get a bottle and a couple of glasses."

"That's all right. I'm in no hurry. I'll just have a couple of beers and wait. Come on back down when . . ." Joe paused in mid-sentence, noticing then, that one of Kelly's eyes was red and swollen.

"My god! What happened to you?" he asked.

"Nothing," Kelly said, putting her hand up to cover the eye and making an even more pronounced effort to turn away from him.

"Don't tell me nothing. You've got as big a shiner there as I've ever seen on anyone."

"I have to go. He'll be waiting on his whiskey," Kelly said, starting toward the stairs.

"Who'll be waiting?" Joe asked.

"Just . . . just one of the customers, that's all."

By now, Big Kate had come over to join in the conversation. When she saw Kelly's red and puffed eye, she sucked in her breath through her teeth. "Oh, honey, what happened to you?" Big Kate asked. Did Harley hit you?" Big Kate reached up to touch Kelly's eye, but Kelly pulled away from her.

"No, please, Big Kate," Kelly said. "I don't want any trouble."

"What's going on, Kelly?" Joe asked. He looked upstairs.

"Nothing, really," Kelly answered.

"I'm going up there to tell him his time is up." Big Kate started toward the stairs.

"No, don't!" Kelly said. "It's all right, nothing is going on." She reached out to grab Big Kate. "Nothing, honest. Please, leave it alone. You saw what he did to that cowboy. I wouldn't want him doing anything like that to you."

"Honey, what kind of house would I be running if I didn't look out for my girls? You don't have to go back up there. Not if he's hurting you."

"It'll be all right," Kelly insisted. "I just don't want any more trouble, that's all."

Kelly started for the stairs, but by the time she reached the bottom step, Harley, wearing only his trousers and a gun belt, appeared at the railing on the upper balcony.

"Hey, you! Bitch!" he shouted down at the girl. "I sent you down there to get a bottle of whiskey, not to have a quilting bee. You've been down there long enough. Get back up here!"

"Harley, she's already been up there long enough," Big Kate called up to him.

"What do you mean, she's been up here long enough?"

"Well, you know how it is," Big Kate answered, forcing a laugh. "I mean, Kelly is a working girl. There are other gents in here wantin' her time, too. I can't let one man just have all her time. Why, how'd it be if you were waitin' on her right now?"

"Yeah? Is there anyone down here that's waitin' on her?"

There were nearly a dozen customers standing around in the

open salon, or sitting on one of the sofas with the other girls, but none of them spoke up.

"See what I mean?" Harley asked with an expansive wave of his hand. "They don't nobody but me want her, 'cause she's nothin' but a worthless slut. Now, you get back up here."

Kelly shut her eyes tightly, squeezing out a tear. Joe watched her as she started toward the stairs. She took no more than a couple of steps, then she stopped. "No," she said. "No, I'm not coming back upstairs."

"The hell you ain't. I paid for you! You belong to me."

Kelly clenched her fists and shook her head. "No, I don't belong to you. Your time is up."

"My time is up when I say my time is up."

Kelly put her hand down in a dress pocket, then pulled out two pieces of silver.

"Here is your money," she said. "I'll give it back to you."

Harley pulled his pistol and pointed it toward Kelly.

"I don't want my money, bitch. I want you. Now you get back up here or else I'm goin' to put a bullet right between your eyes."

"Kelly, if you're not busy now, I'd like a little of your time," Joe said. He spoke the words as calmly as if he had just come into the house, as if none of this drama was being played. He had not said anything before now, because he figured that if Kelly was dumb enough to voluntarily go back upstairs, then he wasn't going to try and stop her. But if she didn't want to go up, he was feeling just contrary enough to see to it that she didn't have to.

Harley looked toward Joe. When he recognized him, his face twisted into a grotesque smile.

"Well, if it isn't Mr. Coulter. I thought the Cattlemen's Association hired you and your brother to hunt down rustlers. Why aren't you out doing your job?"

"My brother is on the job. I decided to come in for a drink," Win said. "And maybe spend a little time with a woman."

"Yeah? Well, not with this woman. She's comin' back up to me."

"I don't think she wants to do that, and as a matter of fact, I don't want her to do it either."

"What the hell do I care what she wants?" Harley sneered. "She's got no choice. Neither do you, Mister Joe Coulter. It *is* Joe, isn't it? I know all about you Coulter brothers. Win is the oldest, and he is the fastest with a gun. You are the biggest, and the fastest with your fists. But your fists aren't going to do you any good, right now, Joe Coulter. You may have noticed that I happen to be holding a gun in my hand."

"Oh, yeah, I see the gun," Joe said. "But what are you going to do with it?"

"What do you mean what am I going to do with it?" Harley answered, obviously exasperated by Joe's question.

"The gun is pointing at the girl," Joe said. "But she's not your problem . . . I am. If you move it toward me, I'm going to kill you. If you shoot her, I'm going to kill you. If you so much as twitch, I'm going to kill you. The only way you are going to get out of this alive is to drop your gun, right now."

"What?" Harley asked in disbelief. "Are you crazy?"

"Oh, you're right, by the way, about my brother being faster with a gun than I am. Now me? Well, I'm not all that fast."

Harley's cocky smile broadened.

"But I am fast enough to kill you," Joe added. "So, what will it be? Are you going to drop the gun, or are you going to die?"

With a shout of rage, Harley swung his gun toward Joe and fired. The bullet slammed into the piano just alongside him, causing the strings to hum. At the same time, in one motion, Joe had his own gun out and he fired back just as Harley loosed a second shot.

Harley's second shot smashed into the overhead chandelier, scattering shards of glass, but doing no further damage. He didn't get off a third shot because Joe made his only shot count.

Harley dropped his gun over the rail and it fell with a clatter to the floor, twelve feet below. He grabbed his chest, then turned his hand out and looked down in surprise and disbelief as his palm began filling with his own blood. His eyes rolled back in his head and he pitched forward, crashing through the railing then turning over once in mid-air before he landed heavily on his back alongside his dropped gun.

Harley lay motionless on the floor with open, but sightless eyes staring toward the ceiling. Big Kate's patrons had scattered when the first shot was fired, but now they began edging back toward the body. Up on the second floor landing, a half-dozen girls and their customers, in various stages of undress, moved quickly to the smashed railing to look down on the scene.

Gunsmoke from the three charges merged to form a large, acrid-bitter cloud to spread over the salon below, and project its pungent odor into all the rooms above.

"Now, there lies one sonofabitch that needed killing," one of Big Kate's patrons said, kicking gently at Harley's still form with the toe of his dust-covered boot.

The shots had been heard outside and half a dozen people ran into Big Kate's Place to see what had happened. One of those who arrived was Marshal Shelby.

Seeing that the dead man was Harley Claymore, he stopped and shook his head. "I told the son of a bitch this was going to happen," he said. "I just didn't figure it was going to happen so soon." Shelby looked over at Joe, who had already put his gun away and was leaning against the piano. "I won't even ask if you're the one who did it. I figure you're the only one who could have."

"It was a fair fight, Marshal," Big Kate said. And, whereas before those in the saloon had been silent when Shelby attempted to solicit information about the killing of Peabody, everyone who had witnessed this fight were more than willing to testify.

"Damndest thing I ever saw, Marshal. Harley already had his gun out," one of the witnesses said.

"You need someone to give a statement, I'll be willin' to," another added.

"Me too," Big Kate said.

"I don't reckon I'll be needing any statements," the marshal said, smiling at Joe. "I'm not even goin' to ask any questions about this one."

By now all the patrons had gathered around Harley's body and a few of the more curious were even squatting beside it to get a closer look.

"Where you reckon his hat and shirt is?" one of the men asked.

"More'n likely still up in the girl's room," another answered.

"I reckon Doc Claymore will be wantin' his son's stuff," Big Kate said.

Shelby nodded, then sighed. "I sure ain't lookin' forward to tellin' Doc Claymore that his son got himself killed." He pointed to two of the bystanders. "You two men get him over to the undertaker so he can get started on a coffin for him. That is, soon as he finishes the one he's workin' on now."

"We'll take him over there, Marshal, but if this keeps up, I'm thinkin' the undertaker is goin' to have to start puttin' people on."

The two men Shelby assigned to the job picked up Harley's body, one under the shoulders, the other at the feet. Harley sagged badly in the middle and they had to struggle to carry him. A couple of the other patrons held the door open while the two men carried him out across the porch, and down into the street.

"Ladies, and your gentlemen friends," Big Kate said after the body was outside. "I think we all need a drink."

The girls and their customers hurried over to the side bar where Big Kate began pouring. Shelby stepped over to Joe and nodded at the happy throng.

"Hell of a note, isn't it, when a man's death is cause for a celebration?"

"I've got a feeling that someone like Harley would rather go out this way than not be noticed at all," Joe said.

"You're probably right," Shelby replied.

"Joe, I want to thank you for what you did," Kelly said, coming up to him then.

"It needed doin'," Joe replied.

"You're always welcome in my bed, Joe Coulter," Kelly said. "But . . . if you don't mind . . . I think I'm going to ask Big Kate to let me be alone tonight."

"I don't mind," Joe said.

"Well, I guess I'd best be going out to Doc Claymore's ranch to tell him what happened," Shelby said, setting his empty beer mug on the bar.

"You want me to go with you?" Joe asked.

"What?" Shelby replied, surprised that Joe would even make the offer. "Are you serious?"

"Yes, I'm serious."

Shelby shook his head. "No, I don't think that would be a good idea."

"Whatever you say," Joe said, returning to his beer as Shelby left, chuckling in amusement over the offer.

With Harley's body gone and the excitement over, most of the girls and their customers soon returned to the sofas and chairs to resume their drinking and conversation. Whatever subject had held their attention before the shooting, the shooting itself was the theme of all the conversations now. It was played and replayed a dozen times over. Once or twice, a couple of the women approached Joe, signaling that even though Kelly was withholding her services for the night, they were available.

Joe had actually come in tonight for a quiet drink and some time with a woman, but the events of the last several minutes had cooled his ardor. Now, all he wanted to do was have a few drinks and be left alone.

Big Kate, sensing that, made certain that Joe got his wish.

Chapter 12

THE NEXT EVENING THE CATTLEMEN'S ASSOCIATION MET IN an emergency session. Doc Claymore had the floor. The expression on his face was pinched, and drawn with sorrow over the death of his son.

"I know that Harley could sometimes be difficult. But he was my son. And now he's dead, shot down by one of the very men we hired to protect us."

"Claymore, I'm sorry that he was your son. And I'm sorry that you are grieved by this," Vogel said. "But not half an hour before he was killed, Harley shot down one of my best men . . . practically in cold blood."

"Everyone who saw it says it was a fair fight," Claymore said.

"Everyone said what they thought your son wanted them to say because they were afraid of him. Now that he's dead the true story has come out. Harley forced the fight."

"Maybe so, but it was a fight between young, hot-blooded men, and it had nothing at all to do with the problem of rustling. Don't you see what I'm getting at?"

"No, I don't think I do."

"What I mean is, this fight may very well have happened whether Coulter was here or not. It was part of the natural order of things. But Joe Coulter's killing Harley wasn't." Claymore ran his hand through his gray, curly hair. "I don't know, I feel responsible, somehow. I mean, here I am, one of those who brought the Coulters in here and what have they done except create an atmosphere of killing? Why, do you realize that since Win and Joe Coulter arrived there have been ten killings? Ten men dead in just a few days, and one of them is my son.''

"And one of the ten, your son killed," one of the other ranchers pointed out.

"I know, I know," Claymore said. He pinched his nose and was quiet for a moment, as if trying to compose himself. Finally, he sighed. "The point is, whether anyone is sorry to see my son gone or not, you have to admit that ten dead in a few days is unconscionable. And I can't help but believe it is the Coulters' general disregard for life that has created this atmosphere. What manner of beasts have we unleashed on our people?''

"What did you expect, Claymore?" Truelove asked. "Did you expect the rustlers to leave just because we hired someone to root 'em out?''

"I don't know," Claymore replied. He put his hand to his forehead and sat down in his chair. "I don't know what I expected. But I didn't plan on starting a bloodbath. And I didn't plan on losing my son. I truly regret having been a party to the hiring of the Coulter brothers. Now, I know why they are called the Bushwhackers.

"And as for my son? Perhaps I should have done something about him. I just continued to nurture the hope that one day he would stop pretending to be a gunfighter and turn into a productive citizen.''

"For god's sake, Claymore, your son had already killed two people before he shot Peabody. He wasn't *pretending* to be a gunfighter. He *was* one.''

"Yes, as much as I hate to admit it, I suppose he was. That's why I didn't have a funeral for him. I know how all of you felt about him, and I didn't want to put you out by asking you to come. Still, he was my son, and I loved him. I buried him this morning, out at the ranch, alongside his ma.''

"What about you, Vogel? Where are you plannin' on buryin' Peabody?" one of the others asked.

"In Boot Hill tomorrow, just after noon," Vogel answered.

"We don't have a cemetery out at the Rocking V, but I'll be lettin' all the boys off to come into town for the funeral. I've already paid for the coffin and took care of the preacher. He's all set to read over the body."

"Me an' my boys'll be there," Masters said.

"So will we," Baker added.

"Yes, I imagine most of us will be. But, gentlemen, if you don't mind, I'd like to suggest that we get back to the topic of our discussion," Claymore said. "As you know, I am concerned about the bloodshed we've unleashed in our valley and I have a question for this group. Which do we value more? Is it property, or human life?"

"What are you gettin' at?"

"I think it's about time we faced up to our responsibilities. A killing fever has been spread over the land and the Coulters are the ones who brought the fever to us."

"You know, gents, Doc may have a point," Masters said. "When you think about it, we were a pretty peaceful town until the Coulters come along. Ever since they arrived there has been a lot of killing."

"Okay, but let's look at it," Truelove said. "Surely you aren't saying that the men who burned my ranch didn't deserve killing? Or the three who were killed when they came back the second time? Because, those are the only deaths the Coulters are responsible for and as far as I'm concerned, it's good riddance to all of them. And one more thing. Not one cow has been stolen since the Coulters arrived."

"Truelove is right about that, gents. The rustlin' has stopped," Baker said. "You've got to consider that."

"They're afraid to come out at night because they know one of the Coulters might be out there, just like a night hawk, waiting to pounce on them from the dark."

"I know how you men feel," Claymore said. "Hell, if you remember, I was as much for hirin' them as any of you. But now, I'm beginning to wonder if we did the right thing."

"So, where does that leave us?" Masters asked.

"That leaves us with a decision to make," Claymore said.

"Hell, if you're trying to figure out whether or not we should keep them, then I say, let's bring it to a vote. But if we're going to vote, I'm telling you here and now, I'm going to vote yes," Truelove said.

"I am too," Vogel said. "I have to admit that the killing does bother me and I think we should keep an eye on it. But, so far, they haven't killed anyone who didn't need killing." He looked over at Claymore. "I'm sorry, Doc, but from all accounts, that includes your son."

Claymore nodded, but said nothing.

"So, for now, I'd say let's keep them around," Vogel concluded.

"I vote for them to stay," Masters added.

"Me too," Baker said.

"Doc?" Truelove asked. "You're the only one we haven't heard from.

Claymore sighed. "All right, I suppose I'll vote to keep them too," he agreed. "I just hope we aren't making a big mistake."

Truelove smiled. "Then it is unanimous. The Coulters stay on the job."

Win and Joe were unaware that the Cattlemen's Association was conducting a meeting to decide their fate. Even if they had been aware, they would have been unconcerned. They were men with a singleness of purpose and their purpose was to break up the rustling ring and bring in Potter. They were going to do that now, regardless of whether or not they had the endorsement of the Association.

Though they kept their rooms at Big Kate's Place, they found that they were actually spending most of their nights out on the prairie. That was because the people they were chasing did most of their work at night, and if they wanted to catch them, they had to be out there with them.

Joe killed a rabbit and spitted it over an open flame to cook for their supper. It was during supper that Win realized they were being watched.

"Joe," he said. "We've got company."

Joe nodded, but said nothing. Then, showing no sign that they knew that anyone was out there, they extinguished the fire, then spread out their bedrolls as if they were about to go to bed. They carefully placed their boots at the foot of the bedroll, and their hats at the top. After that they crawled down into the blankets and lay there for a moment, in the darkness.

"You ready, Joe?" Win whispered.

"I'm ready," Joe whispered back.

Quietly, the two brothers snaked their way out of their bedrolls, then slid down into a small gully that ran adjacent to their camp. Pulling their pistols, they teased the hammers back, then inched up to the top of the gully to stare through the darkness toward the bedrolls.

From there, with their boots and hats in position, it looked exactly as if they were still in the blankets, sound asleep. Win smiled in grim approval. If the campsite looked that way to him, it would look that way to whoever was dogging them.

They waited.

Out on the prairie a coyote howled.

An owl hooted.

A falling star flashed across the dark sky.

A soft, evening breeze moaned through the mesquite.

And still they waited.

Almost a full hour after Win and Joe had "gone to bed," the night was lit up by the great flame-patterns produced by the discharge of a couple of shotguns. The double roar of the shotguns boomed loudly, and Win saw dust and bits of cloth fly up from the bedrolls where charges of buckshot tore into them. Had he and Joe been there, the impact debris would have been bone and flesh rather than dust and cloth, and they would be dead men.

"Now!" Win shouted.

At Win's shout, he and Joe shot in the direction of the muzzle flashes.

"Oh, you sons of bitches! You're a couple of smart ones, you are," a voice shouted, almost jovially. The voice was not near the muzzle flash and Win knew that their would-be assailants must have fired and moved. Whoever they were, they weren't amateurs.

Even as Win thought this, he realized that the assailants could use the flame pattern from their own pistols as targets.

"Joe, move!" he shouted, as he threw himself to the right,

just as the shotguns roared a second time. Though none of the pellets hit them, they dug into the earth where the two brothers had been but an instant earlier and sent a spray of stinging sand into his face. Win fired again, again aiming at the muzzle-blast, though by now he knew there would be no one there. A moment later he heard the sound of retreating hoof beats and he knew that their attackers were riding away.

"You hit, Joe?"

"No. You?"

"No."

"Who do you think it was?"

"My guess is, it has to be a couple of Potter's men," Win answered.

As Spahn and Cain approached the entrance the Hidden Canyon, Spahn removed his hat, then waved it broadly across the top of his head. He put it on, then took it off and repeated the gesture. A moment later they saw a flashing mirror, indicating that they could proceed. When they reached the inner-most part of the valley, they saw a bull-like man with a bald head and a heavy, hairless brow, waiting for him.

"Hello, Potter," Spahn said. "Surprised to see us?"

"No," Potter answered. "I heard about Claymore gettin' his fool self shot down."

"After all the time we wasted with that son of a bitch, for him to go and do a dumb thing like that," Spahn said.

One of the women of the outlaws' camp squealed happily, and came running toward Spahn.

"It wasn't a waste of time. You boys done a good job of keepin' us up on what was goin' on," Potter said. "What about the Coulters?"

Cain shook his head. "They're a couple of smart critters, all right. We trailed 'em last night, and I thought we had them, but they tricked us."

Had any of the range cowboys, or anyone from town, been present now, they would have been shocked by what they were seeing. Gone were the groveling personalities Angus Spahn and Deekus Cain had adopted.

"So, what do you want us to do now?" Spahn asked. "Stay or go back outside?"

"I don't know, I haven't decided yet. Let me think on it a while."

"You had breakfast, Angus?" the woman who was hanging on Spahn asked.

"No."

"Come with me. I'll take care of you."

The woman made no offer to feed Cain, and as Spahn walked away with her, he showed no concern for the fact that his friend hadn't eaten either.

Such behavior didn't bother Cain though. Had the situation been reversed, he would have done the same thing. Without giving it a second thought, he walked over toward the fire where a large, blue-steel coffeepot hung by a wire. Picking up a chipped and stained cup, he bumped the dust out of it, then tipped the pot over to pour a stream of thick, black liquid. As he raised the cup to his lips and blew on the steaming coffee, he looked around.

"Where's Rosa?"

"Rosa?"

"Yeah, you know the one. Big black eyes? She was Johnny Simmons's girl."

"Oh, yeah, I know the one you mean," Potter said. "She's over there, by that kettle. Don't know why you're interested, though. She's still cryin' over Johnny gettin' hisself killed the other night."

"I know. But she's goin' to need someone to comfort her. It might as well be me." Even as Cain spoke, Rosa caught his glance and smiled coquettishly back at him. "See what I mean?" he said, starting toward her.

It wasn't Cain's looks or personality that Rosa was attracted to. With Johnny dead, she had no sponsor. There was no charity in the outlaw camp. Everyone had to pull their own weight, or else have a personal sponsor, or they couldn't stay. And, though no one had told her directly, Rosa was smart enough to realize that it was unlikely anyone who knew as much about the outlaws as she knew, would be allowed to just leave.

An hour later, behind a rock outcropping, Cain was looking down at Rosa as he pulled his pants back on. Rosa hadn't taken her clothes off, but had merely pulled her dress up. Her dress was still bunched around her waist, as she made no effort to cover herself. Her head was turned to one side, and she was crying softly.

"What the hell you crying for?" Cain asked gruffly.

"For no reason," Rosa answered. "Sometimes, a woman cries for no reason." She couldn't tell him that his rough, unskilled lovemaking just underscored how much she would miss Johnny Simmons.

"Deekus?" Spahn called, coming toward them. When Spahn saw Rosa lying on the ground behind the rock, he chuckled. "You finished?"

"Yeah," Cain answered. "What is it?"

"Potter has a job for us."

There were several men gathered around Potter when Spahn and Cain walked up to join them.

"You get your business finished?" Potter asked Cain. The others sniggered knowingly.

"Yeah," Cain answered gruffly.

"Good," Potter said. Then, addressing all of them, Potter continued. "Boys, we're goin' to pay a visit to the Rocking V. I figure we'll drop in along about noon . . . when everyone on the ranch is in town at the cemetery, buryin' that cowboy that Claymore shot. There won't be a livin' soul left out at the ranch. We can just ride in and help ourselves to as many cows as we want to drive away."

Clete Rawlings chuckled. "Yeah," he said. "Yeah, that's a good idea. I got to hand it to you, Potter. Takin' them cows is goin' to be as easy as takin' candy from a baby."

Chapter 13

THE SUN WAS HIGH OVERHEAD AT THE ROCKING V RANCH, A brilliant white orb fixed in the bright blue sky in such a position as to take away all the spots of shade where the cattle would normally congregate. With the shade denied them, the cows had all moved down to mill about in and along the banks of Stillwater Creek.

Stillwater Creek was what made the Rocking V a ranch instead of a stretch of barren desert. Some of the cows had come to water, while others were there just to be nearer the band of green grass that followed the stream on its zig-zagging path across the otherwise brown floor of the valley.

The main building and the outhouses of the ranch sat empty under the blows of the midday sun. Everyone on the ranch, Vogel's family and all his hands, had gone into town for Peabody's funeral. Peabody had been a man who never made more work for others by shirking his own responsibilities. As a result he was well liked by everyone who knew him. Almost as if it were out of respect for him, the ranch was quiet, with even the dogs and chickens maintaining their silence.

Potter was right when he said that every hand on the place would be in town for Peabody's funeral. He was wrong, however, when he said that there wouldn't be a soul on the place. Anticipating exactly what Potter had in mind, Win and Joe were waiting for them. The only question was, from which way would they come? To cover that, Win sent Joe to the north side of the ranch, while he waited on the south. The size of the ranch was such that they were about three miles apart, too far to signal each other by any means other than gunshot, which they didn't want to do because that would give away their positions.

Win was standing on a rock, sucking on the sweet root of a stem of grass, when he saw four men come riding in, moving across the valley floor as leisurely as if they had all day to accomplish their job.

As Win watched their approach, he thought of how easy it would be to set up an ambush. From this angle and range he could cut down a couple of them before they had any idea what was going on. Then he could take out the remaining two before they had time to get away. He knew he wasn't going to do that though. It would stick in his craw.

Win jumped down from the rock, then rode toward the stream where nearly a hundred cows were watering. He chose a route of approach that protected him from observation by a long finger of ridge line that ran parallel to Stillwater Creek.

"How many are we goin' to cut out?" he heard one of the rustlers ask.

"Well, they's four of us. We should be able to drive 'em all . . . at least the ones that's right here," another answered.

"You know, this beats it though. I mean, I went into this business in the first place 'cause I didn't want to punch cows, and what am I doin'? I'm punchin' cows."

The others laughed, then one of them answered, "Yeah, but our cut is a dollar a head for ever'one of these cows we move. You know any cowboys who are makin' that kind of money?"

"No, I reckon not."

They were close enough now that Win could hear them quite clearly. That meant they were close enough to confront. He crested the ridge. There, no more than twenty yards in front of him, he saw the four riders getting ready to move in on Vogel's cows. He pulled his pistol.

"Why don't you fellas just hold it right there?" he called.

"What the hell? Where'd you come from?" Potter hissed, startled by Win's sudden appearance.

"Well, Spahn and Cain," Win said. "I see you didn't take long to find somebody new to suck up to."

The two erstwhile Claymore riders glared at him, but said nothing.

"Shuck your guns and raise your hands," Win said. "We're goin' into town."

"For what?" Cain asked. "We ain't doin' nothin' but takin' a ride."

Suddenly there was an angry buzz, then the "thocking" sound of a heavy bullet tearing into flesh. A fountain of blood squirted up from the neck of Win's horse and the animal went down on its front knees, then collapsed onto its right side. It was almost a full second after the strike of the bullet before the heavy boom of a distant rifle reached Win's ears.

The fall pinned Win's leg under his horse. He also dropped his pistol on the way down, and now it lay just out of reach of his grasping fingers.

"What the hell? Who's that shooting?" Cain shouted, pulling hard on the reins of his horse who, though not hit, was spooked by the sight of seeing Win's horse go down. "Is it one of our men? Who is it?"

"Who the hell cares?" Spahn shouted back. "Look at him! Coulter is pinned down. Here's my chance to kill the son of a bitch!" He raised his gun and fired at Win.

Though Win's right leg was still pinned, he was able to flip his left leg over the saddle and lay down behind his horse, thus providing him with some cover. Spahn's bullet dug into his saddle and sent up a little puff of dust, but did no further damage.

"Shit!" Spahn said. "I can't get to him from this angle."

"Come on!" Cain called. "Let's get the hell out of here while the getting is good!"

"Not until I put a bullet in Coulter!" Spahn insisted. He slapped his legs against the side of his horse and moved around to get a better shot at Win.

Win made one more desperate grab for his pistol but it was still out of reach. His rifle, however, was in the saddle sheath on the side of the horse which was on the ground and Win could see about six inches of the stock sticking out. He grabbed it and was gratified when it pulled free. He jerked it from the sheath and jacked a shell into the chamber, just as Spahn came around to get into position to shoot him.

"Goodbye, Mr. Coulter," Spahn said, raising his pistol and taking careful aim. The smile left his face as he saw the business end of Win's rifle raise up, then spit a finger of flame. The .44-40 bullet from Win's rifle hit Spahn just under the chin, then exited the back of his head along with a pink spray of blood and bone as Spahn tumbled off his horse.

"He got Spahn!" one of the men said.

"That's his own damn fault. Let's get the hell out of here!" Cain shouted.

Cain and the two men with him were riding away hard now, not even bothering to look back to see what happened to Spahn. In the meantime, another bullet whistled by from the distant rifle. When Win located the source of the shooting, he saw a mounted man with one leg thrown casually across his saddle. Using that leg to provide a stable firing platform, the shooter raised his rifle to fire again. There was a flash of light, the man rolled back from the recoil, then the bullet whizzed by so close to Win's head that it made his ears pop. All this before the report of the rifle actually reached him. With a gasp of disbelief, Win realized that this man was firing from at least one thousand yards away! Win fired back, not with any expectation of actually hitting his target, but merely to show his enemy that he wasn't completely helpless.

In a way, Win was running a bluff, because he *was* practically helpless. He was still trapped under his horse and he knew if he didn't get himself free soon, whoever was shooting at him would be able to change locations and catch Win in an exposed position. Win tried again to pull his leg free but he was unable to do so. Then he got an idea. He stuck the stock of the rifle just under the horse's side and grabbed the barrel. Using the rifle as a lever, he pushed up and wedged just enough space between the horse's flesh and the ground to allow him to slip his leg free.

His first fear was that his leg might be broken, but as soon as he pulled it out, he knew that it wasn't. The blood circulation was cut off however, and when he tried to stand he promptly fell back down again. As it was, that turned out to be a blessing, for another bullet whistled by at that very moment, at the precise place where his head would have been, had he been standing.

Crawling on his belly, Win slithered and twisted his way down to the stream. He reached the bank, then got down into the water just as another bullet ploughed into the dirt beside him. Win twisted around behind the bank and looked back up toward the place where the shots were coming from. With the stream bank providing him cover and a rifle in his hands, he was no longer a sitting duck. Whoever was after him realized this as well, for Win saw him put his rifle back in the saddle sheath, then turn and ride away as casually as if he were riding down main street. And why not? There was no way Win was going to hit him at this distance, at least not with a .44-40 Winchester.

Win heard the hooves of a fast approaching horse, and he turned quickly to confront the new challenge. He breathed a sigh of relief, however, when he saw that it was Joe.

"Win! Are you all right?" Joe called.

"Yeah," Win called back. He pointed to Spahn's horse which had trotted away during the shooting but was back now, peacefully cropping grass. "Grab that horse, Joe. I'll need a mount."

"What happened?" Joe asked a moment later as he returned with Spahn's horse.

As Win switched his saddle with Spahn's, he told Joe about the long distance shooter.

"Was he one of Potter's men?" Joe asked.

"I don't think so," Win replied. "They ran from him."

"Well, that's strange. Who the hell would be shooting at both of you?"

"Whoever he is, he's one hell of a shot," Win said.

Once they were mounted, they rode up to the top of the distant ridge to the spot where the shooting had come from. Win wanted to have a look at the place where the gunman had been.

A flash of sunlight led him to the first sign. When he picked it up he saw that it was the brass casing of a .45-caliber shell of a type made especially for the Whitworth. The Whitworth, Win knew, was a hexagonal-shaped, long-barrel rifle which, when fitted with a telescope, could be fired accurately at ranges up to 1,000 yards. It had been the preferred weapon of the long-distance sharpshooters during the War between the States.

"You know anybody who owns such a gun?" Joe asked.

Win shook his head. "No, I don't. But if I ever see one sticking out of a saddle sheath, I plan to ask a few questions."

Laying aside the puzzle of who the long-distance shooter had been, the two brothers rode back down to where Spahn's body lay sprawled in death. Joe picked the rustler up and threw him across the saddle pommel in front of Win. Then they rode into town with him.

Boot Hill was located at the western end of town. Wagons and buggies were leaving the cemetery as the friends of Earl Peabody began returning to their own lives. The funeral service for Peabody was just breaking up as the Coulters rode into town.

"That's eleven," someone said quietly as he saw Win and Joe ride by with Spahn's body draped across Win's horse. "Eleven men have been killed since the Bushwhackers arrived in town."

Marshal Shelby stood on the little wooden sidewalk just in front of his office as Win flipped Spahn's body off. Spahn landed on his back in the dirt of the street, sending up a little cloud of dust. Several people were nearby and a few of them came over to stare at Spahn's body. His eyes were open and glazed, there was a small, black hole just under his chin, and a much larger one, with blood-matted hair, at the back of his head.

"It's Spahn," word went on down the street. Within moments, others were coming toward the marshal's office, anxious to get a look at the latest victim of the rapidly escalating death toll.

"You sort of wasted your time with that one, didn't you, Coulter?" the marshal said. "Spahn's no rustler. He rides for Doc Claymore."

"Not since yesterday, he didn't. He *was* ridin' for Doc Claymore, but after Harley got hisself killed, Spahn and Cain both quit," someone in the crowd said.

"Yeah, they didn't have Harley's ass to kiss anymore," one of the others said, and there was a nervous tittering of laughter.

Doc Claymore pushed his way through the crowd and looked down at Spahn's body, then up at Win and Joe.

"What'd you shoot him for? He was as harmless as they come. Why, without my son to tag along after, I doubt this boy could even go to the bathroom by himself."

"This 'boy,' as you call him, tried to kill me," Win said. "I killed him in self-defense. I had no choice."

"Why, he and Cain were afraid of their own shadows. It is hard for me to picture him throwing down on anyone. Especially going up against someone like you," Claymore said in a voice that indicated he didn't believe Win. "What do you suppose would make him do such a thing?"

"Let's just say that he found himself in what he thought was an advantageous position," Win explained. "Turns out he was wrong."

"I see. Uh, Mr. Coulter, perhaps it's about time we had a little talk. Just you, your brother, me, and the Cattlemen's Association." Looking around, Claymore saw Vogel, True-love, Baker and Masters in the crowd, and nodding at them, he invited them in to be a party to the conversation.

The Cattlemen's Association had its office next door to the marshal's office. The office had been closed during Peabody's funeral and the men had to wait for a moment while Doc Claymore unlocked the door. Once inside, they took their usual seats around the long conference table, with Doc Claymore in his position at the head, as the Association's president. As the office had been closed up for most of the day, it was quite hot and stuffy. One of the men raised a window to let in some air, and with the air came the odor of horse droppings from the street. To most of the townspeople the street odors were as unnoticable as the other odors of the town . . . the rotting garbage, the stale beer and whiskey from behind the saloons, the several dozen outhouses which reeked in the mid-day sun. To Win and Joe, who were used to the wide-open spaces, the smells of civilization were overpowering.

Doc Claymore took out a handkerchief and wiped his face, then pointed to a couple of chairs, inviting the boys to be seated. Joe sat, but Win declined, leaning instead against the wall. He took out the makings and started rolling a cigarette.

"Is there a problem?" Win asked.

The others looked at Claymore, not only because he was the head of the Association, but because he was the one who had called the meeting.

Claymore drummed his fingers on the table for a moment, then answered Win's question.

"Yes, Mr. Coulter, there *is* a problem. We've already had one meeting to discuss the situtation and events are dictating that we have another. I have to tell you that we of the Association, as well as many of the citizens of the town, are becoming quite concerned with what seems to be an excessive amount of bloodshed. Every reward that the Association has paid so far has been paid for a body. Not once since you two arrived has a living prisoner been brought in for reward. That, despite the fact that the reward is just as high for those you bring in alive, as it is for those you bring in dead."

"We haven't killed anyone who wasn't trying to kill us," Win said. "And they have all been rustlers . . . the very people you are paying us to hunt down."

"What about my son?" Claymore asked. "He certainly wasn't a rustler. And neither was Spahn."

"I'm sorry about your son," Joe said. "But I didn't have any choice. He was trying to kill me."

"I know, I've heard from all the witnesses," Claymore said. "And much as it pains me to believe them, I do believe them. If I didn't believe them, you may rest assured, Mr. Coulter, that you would be dead by now."

"Your son may not have been a rustler, but I believe Spahn was," Win said. "I killed him on Vogel's ranch. And he was riding with three other men. There's no doubt in my mind but that they were out there to steal Vogel's cattle while everyone was at the funeral."

"Damn!" Vogel said, slamming his fist into his open hand.

"Coulter's right, Doc. It all makes sense. Of course the bastards would choose today to come."

"But Spahn?"

"He and Cain must've joined up with Potter," Vogel said. "Hell, you said it yourself, they both quit right after Harley was killed. And neither one of them had the gumption to do anything on their own. Hell they could be led around like a couple of puppy dogs."

"Just because a man lacks gumption, that shouldn't be enough cause to get him shot," Claymore said.

"I'm not sure that you knew Spahn and Cain as well as you thought you did," Win said.

"What do you mean?"

"The Spahn I saw out there on the range was not the poltroon you have been portraying. He was tough, vicious, and determined. He wanted to kill me, and he came at me, head on."

The ranchers laughed.

"To what do you attribute Spahn's sudden conversion from a coward to a warrior?"

"That's just it," Win said. "I don't think it was a sudden change."

"What do you mean?"

"I think he was always the man I saw. I think he was acting the part of a toady. I think he and Cain took all of you in. I think they were both working for Potter all along."

"You're just saying that, because you want to be paid for one more body," Doc Claymore suggested. "You've overstepped your bounds, Coulter. Both of you have. And I think we should discuss whether or not we are going to continue this arrangement."

"I don't," Truelove said.

"What do you mean?" Claymore asked, surprised by the comment.

"Doc, this is the second time you've called a meeting about this," Truelove said. "Now, we voted to keep them the last time and I'm willin' to bet we're going to vote to keep them this time. The truth is, I'm gettin' tired of holdin' a meeting every time someone gets themselves shot. I say they're doing a good job and I say let's leave them alone.''

"I agree," Baker said, and Vogel concurred.

"Am I the only one worried about the excessive amount of killing going on around here?" Doc Claymore asked.

"As far as I'm concerned, it's not excessive as long as it's needed," Truelove said.

"But are we sure that it's needed?"

"We don't have any reason to believe that it isn't."

Doc Claymore sighed and leaned back in his chair. He pressed his hands together and studied Win and Joe for a long time before he spoke.

"Very well, we'll keep you on. However, for my own peace of mind, could I have your assurances that no more people will be killed?"

"I'm sorry, but we can't promise that," Win said.

"Then can I have your word that no more will be killed than is absolutely necessary?"

"I've already given my word on that," Win said. "I see no reason to do it again."

"He's right, Doc," Truelove said. "I told you, let's just leave them alone and let them go about their business."

"I agree with Truelove," Masters said.

"Vogel? Baker?"

"I think they are doing a bang-up job," Vogel said.

"They've my vote," Baker added.

"All right, all right, I'll go along with the majority." Claymore agreed. "But I want it clearly understood that I am on record as abhorring all the violence which I believe these men have spawned."

"We'll keep that in mind," Truelove said.

"Is that all?" Win asked.

"Yes."

"Good."

"All I have to say to you men is, keep up the good work," Vogel said. "If you hadn't been on the job, I would have lost a sizeable part of my herd."

"Yeah. I guess we owe you an apology and our thanks," Baker suggested.

Chapter 14

"BEANS AGAIN!" RAWLINGS GROWLED AS THE FAT MEXICAN woman spooned them onto his plate. "Is that all you ever have around here?"

"We have no more beef, señor," the cook said. "And the bacon, she is gone too."

"Well, now, this is a hell of a note, ain't it?" Rawlings complained as he walked over to sit at the rough-hewn table with half a dozen other men. "I mean we've rustled enough beef to start a full-sized stampede, but we ain't got so much as a mouthful of meat to lay alongside our beans."

"Quit your belly-achin'," Potter growled as he held his own plate out. "If you want meat for every meal, you can always go back to punchin' cows for thirty dollars a month and found. You're rustlin' cows because it pays more, not because it's an easy life."

"Perhaps you ain't noticed it lately, Potter, but we ain't exactly been rustlin' a hell of a lot of cows, either. In fact, it's been quite a while since we've so much as took one steer and got away with it."

"Yeah," a man named Wilson put in. "You said it'd be a piece of cake to go out to Truelove's place and take his herd. Well, we went out there. And we lost five men burnin' the place down and another three when we raided the ranch. They was good men too, ever' one of 'em. All that and for what? We didn't get so much as one cow."

"And we didn't get nothin' from the Rocking V, either, except Angus got hisself killed," Cain added.

"You got no room to talk, Cain," Potter growled. "You 'n Spahn lived the good life for a long time while we was in here livin' on beans and spit."

"What we need to do is get rid of the Coulter brothers," a man named Morgan suggested.

"The problem is, the Coulters ain't our only problem," Rawlings suggested. "Don't forget the son of a bitch who was shootin' at us from damn near a mile away."

"That was probably the other Coulter brother," Wilson said. "There's two of 'em, remember, and we only had one of 'em trapped."

Rawlings shook his head. "No. Whoever it was that shot at us, was shootin' at Coulter too. Don't you remember? He's the one that killed Coulter's horse."

"Yeah, that's true, isn't it?" Wilson said, stroking his chin. "Well, I'm wondering now, just who that could be?"

"Well, whoever he was, he isn't our biggest problem. Our biggest problem is still the Coulters. They have just about brought our rustlin' days to a halt," Rawlings said.

"It don't seem right that no more'n a couple of ordinary men could do that to us," Wilson complained.

"Well, see, now there's the problem," Morgan said. "The Bushwhackers ain't exactly what would you call ordinary men."

"What do you mean?" Wilson asked.

"What I mean is, they're more like ghosts than regular men," Morgan explained. "I mean, no matter where we go, they are there first . . . comin' in as silent as smoke, raisin' hell, then goin' away without so much as a scratch for all the shootin'."

"They've just been lucky so far, that's all."

"Lucky hell," Morgan replied. "Luck ain't got nothin' to do with it. I'm here to tell you, they ain't no ordinary men."

"Problem with you, Morgan, is they've got you spooked bad," Rawlings said. Rawlings looked over at Potter. "You've met them, Cain. What do you think about what Morgan said?"

Cain spooned some beans onto his folded tortilla, then took

a bite and chewed thoughtfully before he answered. "What do I think?" he repeated "I think Morgan was right when he said we need to kill the sons of bitches. That's what I think."

"Easy enough to say . . . not so easy to do," Morgan said. "I don't figure either one of the Coulters are the kind of man that dies easy."

"Bullshit. Put a bullet in their hide and they'll die just like ever'one else," Potter growled.

"Then how come we ain't been able to kill them?"

"We haven't tried," Potter said. "Except for Harley Claymore and Angus Spahn. And they don't count for much, because one of them was a blowhard and the other was a damn fool."

"Are you sayin' that *you'd* be willin' to go up against either one of them?" Wilson asked Potter.

"Hell, no," Potter answered. "I ain't willin' to go up against them and I don't figure anybody else should have to, either."

"What do you mean? I thought you said they needed killin'."

"They *do* need killin'," Potter said. He smiled. "But what does goin' up against them have to do with it? What the hell, we don't need to make no sportin' contest out of this. We ain't like that fool Harley Truelove, tryin' to be known as the 'Fastest Gun in the West.' There don't none of us need to try it alone, and there ain't no need to face either one of them sons of bitches down. I mean, all that's needed is for someone to kill the bastards. If they're shot in the front or in the back, it don't make no difference. They'll be just as dead."

"Yeah," one of the others said. "Sneak up on the sons of bitches and shoot 'em in the back. That's the way to handle him."

"I got an idea how maybe to get this done," Potter said, wiping some of the dripping bean juice from his chin. "S'pose we all put one hundred dollars in a pot, just like as if we was playin' poker. If one man kills one of the Coulters, half the money is his. If he kills both of 'em, all the money is his. And, if more than one winds up doin' it, then they'll split up the money."

"Yeah, that sounds like a good idea," Wilson said. He stuck his hand into his pocket and pulled out a wad of bills. "Ante up, fellas. I don't need anybody to help me, the way I'm goin' to it. And if I am the one that kills them both, then I want to see how much money I'm goin' to get."

Some distance away, a small man with blotchy red skin, watery blue eyes and a prominent hook nose was just approaching the town of Sulphur Springs. The sun was down now, and the night creatures were calling to each other. A cloud passed over the moon, then moved away, bathing in silver the little town that rose up before him. Two dozen buildings, half of which spilled yellow light onto the ground out front, faced the town's single street. The biggest building at this edge of town was the livery stable, dark inside, though lighted from without by the town's only street lamp. The most brightly lit building was the town saloon.

The man, whose name was Jarred Snell, stopped his horse just at the edge of a little stand of cottonwood trees, then ground-hobbled him. He pulled his long-barreled Whitworth from the saddle sheath then unwrapped the special oiled cloth he kept around it. The hexogonal barrel gleamed in the moonlight as Snell opened the breach and slid in the long, conical cylinder that made up the bullet and casing to which the rifle had been adapted from its original ball-and-cap mechanism.

Snell was only five feet two inches tall and weighed just under 130 pounds. However, he rode a very large horse . . . the big black stallion standing at least two hands higher than average. The result of this unlikely combination was to make Snell look even smaller and his horse even larger than they actually were.

In the Louisiana bayou country where Snell grew up, his diminutive size had been quite a disadvantage. Strength, and the ability to use one's fists, were what established the hierarchy of the bayou. Bullied by those who were larger than he, Snell's earlier years were shadowed by intimidation and shame. Then one day, in desperation, Snell grabbed a shotgun and blew a hole in the guts of one of his tormentors.

No one else in the bayou had ever seen an argument settled

by any means other than sheer strength. When they saw the strongest of their number brought down by the weakest, they were visibly frightened and they began to give Snell a new and unexpected respect. Shortly thereafter, that respect manifested itself in Snell's being elected to the position of Lieutenant in the Bayou Bengals, a regiment of Louisiana volunteers, organized to fight in the civil war.

During the war Snell discovered two things about himself. He learned that he had no compunctions about pulling the trigger, and he discovered that he liked the feeling of power he experienced by seeing others cowering before him. It was a feeling he didn't intend to surrender ever again.

While others cursed the war, Snell enjoyed it. It was as if society had created an environment just for him. He could kill as often as he wanted, and as long as the men he killed wore a different color uniform from the one he was wearing, he would be honored, instead of condemned.

It was the best thing that had ever happened to him, but when the war was over he found himself without an avocation. Then he discovered a trade that would allow him to continue to use his skill. He became a bounty hunter, specializing only in the most desperately wanted men, the "Dead or Alive" cases. This way he could kill without compunction—and without fear of punishment—while also being paid for it. It was as if the business had been developed especially for him.

When reward posters were circulated on Emil Potter and members of his band of rustlers, Snell came to Paso del Muerte to ply his avocation. When he made inquiries about Potter and his gang, he was told that the Cattlemen's Association had entered into an agreement with Win and Joe Coulter.

"Is the Cattlemen's Association in the habit of hiring wanted men?" Snell asked.

"Wanted men?"

Snell produced an old, yellowed poster on the Coulters.

WANTED
DEAD OR ALIVE
For Murder and Mayhem

By the State of Kansas
WIN AND JOE COULTER
Also Known As
the Bushwhackers
$1,500 for Each

"Why, that circular is several years old," Snell was told.

"Don't matter none. There's no statute of limitations on murder," Snell replied.

The situation now seemed made-to-order for Snell. He could not only eliminate his competition, he could get paid for it. He made an attempt at one of the Coulters and had missed. He planned to try again, but not just yet. He needed to back away a bit, to give the Coulters time to let their guard down again. Snell was most deadly when the element of surprise was on his side.

Snell had a unique way of operating his business. He called it "running a trap line." By putting out the proper bait, he could reasonably expect his quarry to show up in one of his traps.

The saloon in Sulphur Springs was one such trap. Snell let it be known that an accomplice was needed for an easy payroll robbery. Anyone interested in the job was to walk out of the saloon at exactly nine o'clock in the evening on this very day, come to the lamppost by the stable, and examine his pocket watch. That would be the signal by which they would meet. Further arrangements would be concluded at that time.

Earlier that day, Snell learned that someone had, indeed, taken the bait. It was Arnold Fenton. Though Fenton had been a small fry up until now, he had recently killed a bank teller in a botched hold-up attempt, and was now worth $1,000, "Dead or Alive." For someone like Jarred Snell, collecting that $1,000 would be as easy as picking an apple from a tree.

Inside the saloon, Arnold Fenton stood at the bar nursing a beer. He had come in with just enough money for a beer and a plate of beans. He had nearly been killed during his last robbery attempt, and hadn't gotten one red cent for his troubles. He wished he had enough money to go into the back

room with one of the two women who were working the bar,
but he didn't. He didn't even have enough money for a second
beer.

If everything worked out though, that would soon change.
Fenton was here to meet a man to plan a job. After that, his
pockets would be full again. He looked over at the wall clock.

"Is your clock right?" he asked the bartender.

The bartender, who was busy polishing glasses, set the
towel down and pulled out his watch. He flipped open the case
and looked at it, then glanced back at the clock.

"Yes, sir," he said. "It is lacking five minutes of nine
o'clock."

"Thanks," Fenton replied.

"Would you like another beer, sir?"

"No, thank you. Not just yet," Fenton answered.

"Very good, sir."

The bartender went back to wiping glasses. Fenton raised
his nearly empty beer mug. There was just enough beer left
to wet his lips.

According to the instructions, Fenton was to go outside and
stand under the lamppost in front of the livery at exactly nine
o'clock, and examine his pocket watch. He didn't actually
have a pocket watch—he had sold it long ago. But he figured
if he pretended to be examining one, it would amount to the
same thing.

He took another swallow of beer, then made a face. He had
been nursing the beer so long that it had gone flat on him. It
was pure hell to be in this world without money. He looked
back toward the Regulator clock and saw the minute hand
move to one minute until nine. He finished his beer, slapped
the mug down, wiped the back of his hand across his mouth
and started for the door.

"Come again," the bartender called to him.

"When you've got more money," one of the bar girls
called. She followed her chiding with a high-pitched laugh.
The man with her guffawed in a rich, bass tone.

"I will," Fenton replied.

Like hell, he thought. When he had enough money he was
going to go to someplace where he could have a good time . . .

someplace like Denver or San Francisco. He wouldn't be caught dead in a place like this.

Snell held a match to his watch face and saw that it was five till nine. He figured that was close enough to the time that it wouldn't be necessary for him to check it anymore. All he would have to do is wait for his man to show, and that should be any time now.

A man came out of the saloon and stepped into the street. He stood there for a moment looking in both directions. Snell raised the rifle to his shoulder and waited. The man looked back toward the saloon and shouted something, then another man came out and the two of them walked together toward the opposite end of the town, away from the stable.

Snell lowered the rifle.

Behind him his horse whickered and stamped its foot.

Somewhere down in the little town, a dog barked.

A back door slammed shut in one of the houses and, in the moonlight, Snell saw a man heading for the toilet, carrying a wad of paper with him.

From the saloon he heard a woman's high-pitched laugh, then the lower guffaw of her companion.

A mule brayed.

Another patron came out of the saloon door and, like the first man, stood for a moment on the street, looking both ways. Snell watched him carefully, then saw him start toward the stable. Again, Snell raised his rifle and pointed it toward the street lamp.

The man stopped under the light of the lamp, reached into his pocket then raised his hand to study it pointedly. Snell aimed at the easy target the street lamp provided for him, squeezed the trigger slowly, then was rocked back by the recoil of the exploding cartridge. Even from here, he could see part of the man's skull fly away as the heavy lead slug crashed through his head.

The heavy boom of the shot rolled back from the distant hills so that it sounded almost like a volley, rather than one exceptionally well-placed shot. Snell mounted his horse and rode quickly toward the sprawled body of the man he had just shot. By the time he reached the stable, more than two dozen townspeople, men, women and children, had poured out of the saloon, the closer houses and other buildings, to gather around the body.

"Who did this?" someone was asking. "Did anybody see anything?"

Snell saw a glint of light on the questioner's chest and realized that it was the reflection of a star. This was the sheriff.

"I did it, Sheriff," Snell said, swinging down from his horse.

"You?" the sheriff asked. His eyes narrowed as he took Snell in, a small man, dressed in black, riding a big black horse with a long rifle sheathed on one side, and a sawed-off shotgun on the other.

"Who the hell are you, Mister? You dry-gulch a man, then just come ridin' in here bold as life and announce you're the one that did it?" He pulled his pistol. "You're under arrest."

"I don't think so," Snell said. He pulled a poster from his shirt pocket and showed it to the sheriff. "Unless I miss my guess, this fella is Arnold Fenton."

The sheriff unfolded the poster and looked at it. He read it quickly, then looked back at Snell. "What do you mean, unless you miss your guess? You mean you ain't sure?"

"Well, I was back up there on the hill," Snell said. "And of course, it being dark and all, I could be mistaken. But I don't think I am."

"My god, mister, you tryin' to tell us you took him down from way back there?"

"If you go back to that stand of cottonwood trees, you'll find the empty shell casing," Snell answered.

"My god, that's over five hundred yards away . . . in the dark," someone said in awe.

"I'm goin' to get me that shell casing," a young boy shouted, and his declaration set in motion half a dozen other young boys, all scampering to be the first to lay claim to the souvenir.

"Anyone know this man?" the sheriff asked.

"It's Arnold Fenton, all right," one of the men who had been drinking with him in the saloon said.

"Well, there you go, Sheriff. Looks like I got the right man after all," Fenton said. "As you can see by the dodger, there's a thousand-dollar reward out on him. Dead or alive," he added pointedly. He nodded toward the hotel. "I'm going to take a room in the hotel for tonight. I expect you'll have verification and payment by noon tomorrow, won't you?"

The sheriff nodded. "I reckon I will," he said. "But, by god, I don't mind tellin' you, somethin' like this sticks in my craw."

"Just have the money," Snell said.

"He sure is full of himself," one of the saloon patrons said as Snell started toward the hotel.

"Shhh!" someone said. "He might hear you."

"What do I care if he hears me? Hell, the little shit wouldn't dress out much over a hundred pounds."

"A rattlesnake isn't very big either," the sheriff pointed out. "But you don't go pissing one of them off, if you can help it."

Back in Paso del Muerte, Win and Joe had answered a summons to come to the Truelove Ranch.

"What do you think?" Truelove asked, pointing to the new house. "Of course, it don't have nothin' but a canvas cover for a roof, but by the time we get a roof on, it'll be as fine as the old one ever was."

"It'll be even better," Martha said, beaming proudly. "I was hoping to get the old house fixed up, or maybe even get a new one. Of course, I never planned on getting it this way," she added.

"You got it built pretty fast," Win said.

"That's the way it is out here when neighbors get together," Truelove said. "Mostly it was the Association."

"Ah, yes, the Association," Win said.

"They've been pretty hard on you boys, haven't they? I apologize for that."

"Don't worry about it. It comes with the territory," Joe said.

"Nevertheless, they're coming at you two like the Spanish

Inquisition or something," Truelove said. "They have no right to question your methods or your motives."

"I appreciate your kind words," Win said.

"Words? Humph. Words are a dime a dozen," Martha replied. "We want you to eat dinner with us."

Joe grinned broadly. "Miz Truelove, I like the way you think," he said.

Dinner was fried chicken, mashed potatoes, fresh butterbeans, biscuits, and gravy. It was topped off with large slices of apple pie.

Ev ate with them. He apologized and explained that as he was the only hand remaining, he had taken to eating with the family. Martha said he was almost like one of the family anyway, and Win noticed in the exchange of glances between Ev and Lucy, that he might, indeed, be a part of the family some day.

"Pa," Lucy said after the dessert was finished, "can we show him now?"

Truelove smiled. "Sure, I guess now's as good a time as any," he said. "Win, if you don't mind, I'd like you come on out to the barn with us. Lucy and Ev have something they want to show you." Truelove looked over at Joe. " 'Course, you can come too, Joe. But this is mostly for Win."

"Well then, if you don't mind, I think I'll just have me another piece of pie," Joe said. He looked at Martha. "That is . . . if it wouldn't be puttin' you out any," he added.

Martha chuckled. "It so happens, Joe, that I held back the largest piece, just in case you would want seconds. Same as before? Topped with a slab of cheese?"

"Yes'm," Joe said. "That was mighty good."

As Joe started on his second piece of pie, Win followed Truelove and the others outside. Ev went into the barn, then, a moment later, came back, leading a big black horse. The horse, which was already saddled, was a magnificent animal, with a coat so lustrous and black that the sunbeams that played off him danced in flashes of blue lightning.

"You'll be needin' a horse to replace the one you got killed," Truelove said.

"Yes," Win said. He pointed to the horse he had ridden out on. "I rented this one from the stable."

"What about this one?"

Win went over to look at the horse more closely. He was a perfect figure of conformation with flared nostrils and eyes that flashed fire.

"You like him?" Lucy asked Win.

"He's about the best-looking piece of horse flesh I've ever seen," Win said, patting him on the neck. "How much are you asking for him?"

"He's not for sale," Truelove said.

"What? But I thought . . ."

"He's yours," Lucy said. "A gift to you from us."

"No," Win replied. "I can't do that. I can't take him for nothing."

"Sure you can," Truelove insisted. Martha and Lucy and Ev and I have already discussed it, and we figured we owe you something for what you did for us . . . not only helping us fight off the raid, but also in letting us claim the reward. You got your horse killed, you need another one, and we want to give this one to you."

"He's a good one," Ev said. "I raised him myself, from a colt. I was going to make him a part of my string, but I think you'll have better use for him."

"Get on him, see how it feels," Truelove suggested.

Win swung up into the saddle, then leaned down and patted the horse on the neck a couple of times.

"Go ahead," Ev said. "Give him a run. I want you to see what you've got."

"All right," Win agreed. "I'll just do that." He slapped his legs against the horse's sides. "Let's go," he said.

The horse burst forward like a cannonball, reaching top speed at once, surprising Win by its immediate response. Win bent low over his withers, feeling the rush of wind in his face and experiencing the pure thrill of the run, feeling almost as if he and the horse were one, sharing the same muscle structure and bloodstream. The horse's hooves drummed a rapid rhythm against the ground and it kicked up little spurts of dust behind him. Win pulled him to a stop and turned him. He was amazed at how far he had come in such a short time. As he returned to the little group in front of the barn, he had a big grin on his face.

"What do you think?" Ev asked.

"I have to tell you, this is more horse than I've ever been on before."

"You'll take him then?" Lucy asked, anxiously.

"Miss Truelove, right now I believe I'd fight anyone who tried to take him away from me," Win replied.

"He's yours," Truelove said. "Come inside and I'll give you a bill of sale."

"I've never given him a name," Ev said. "So you can call him anything you want."

Win smiled. "He doesn't need a name. He knows who he is and I know who I am."

Chapter 15

THREE DAYS LATER WIN AND JOE UNCOVERED WHAT THEY had been looking for. They found the valley where the rustlers were hiding out.

Actually, they were pretty sure of its location even before they found it, because they had already looked up every other valley and draw within thirty miles of Paso del Muerte, and this was the only place left that it could be. Then, when they started exploring this canyon and saw that it had a narrow, easily guarded entrance, they knew they were in the right spot. After that, there was nothing left for them to do but dismount and let their horses crop grass while they sat in the shade and kept watch for a while.

It was mid-afternoon when two riders finally exited the canyon. One was tall and lanky, with a bushy, walrus-type mustache. The other was short and stocky with a scraggly beard.

"Win?" Joe said.

"Yeah, I see them."

"Ever seen 'em before?"

"They were with Cain and Spahn when they tried to hit the Vogel place," Win said.

Win and Joe moved out to a ledge which overlooked the pass, then lay very still as the two rustlers rode right beneath them. They were so close, they could hear the riders as they were talking.

"I tell you, Wilson, we ought not to be doin' this. Potter

ain't goin' to like it much, us ridin' out on our own," the short, stocky rider said.

"He'll calm down when we bring in a side of beef," the tall, lanky one answered. "Come on, Quinn, admit it. Ain't you gettin' damn hungry for somethin' more'n beans and tortilla? Wouldn't a little beefsteak go good now and again?"

"Yeah," Quinn replied. "It would. But I still don't know if this is such a good idea. I mean, planning a job on our own."

"What job?" Wilson replied. "This ain't no job. I mean, we ain't really goin' out to do any rustling or anything. We're goin' to find one cow, that's all. And we ain't even goin' to drive it anywhere. We're goin' to butcher it on the spot and we're goin' to bring back the choice pieces. We'll be back before sundown and have beef in our bellies before we go to sleep."

The two men continued their conversation but they rode out of ear shot so that Win and Joe were no longer able to follow what they were saying. It didn't matter. They didn't have to hear any more . . . they had already heard enough to realize that these two men were acting on their own, and that no one else would be coming out behind them.

Win and Joe hurried back to their horses, mounted, then rode parallel with the two riders while also making a very big circle so as not to be seen by Wilson and Quinn. They put their horses into ground-eating lopes and easily raced ahead of them. Then, a few minutes later, they suddenly appeared on the trail just ahead of the two riders. Startled by their unexpected appearance, both horses reared and Wilson and Quinn had to fight them to bring them under control.

Win and Joe sat there, calmly, patting their own horses reassuringly, so they wouldn't be spooked by the antics of Wilson and Quinn's animals.

"Good evenin' boys," Win said easily.

"Son of a bitch, it's the Coulters! Where'd you two come from?" Quinn shouted. Once he had his horse under control, his shoulder jerked as if he were about to go for his gun, but Win shook his head and cocked the pistol he was already holding in his hand. The metallic sound of the clicking sear as the cylinder rolled into position was cold and frightening, and it stopped Quinn before he made a mistake. Quinn dropped his free arm by his side.

"You two unbuckle your gunbelts and hand them to my brother," Win ordered.

Quinn and Wilson took off their gunbelts then handed them to Joe, who hooked both of them across his saddle pommel.

"What do you want with us?" Wilson asked.

Win waved the barrel of his pistol in a motion to indicate they should get going. "I want you to come along with us," he said.

"Why should we do that?"

"Because, dead or alive, you're money in the bank for us," Joe said. "Now, go ahead, do what my brother said before you get him pissed off."

It was nearly sundown by the time Win and Joe herded their two prisoners into Paso del Muerte. A shimmer of sunlight bounced off the roofs and sides of the buildings, painting the town red as they prodded the prisoners down the street toward the marshal's office.

Next door to the marshal's office was the Cattlemen's Association and across the street from that was the saloon. The boys were thirsty and they could almost taste the beer they would be drinking in a few minutes. Their thirst was heightened by the large sign which the saloon was touting. It was a painting of a golden mug of beer hanging out over the boardwalk, squeaking an invitation as it swung back and forth in the late-afternoon breeze.

They rode straight to the jail. Joe dismounted first, while Win kept an eye on the prisoners. Then with Joe watching them from the ground, Win dismounted.

"Get down, you two," Joe ordered.

Marshal Shelby met them just in front of the door. "Well, here's a change," Shelby said. "You brought me a couple of live ones." Shelby looked at the two prisoners. "Come on in, boys. I think you're going to like it here."

"You think you're going to keep us here, old man?" Quinn asked. "As soon as Potter finds out where we are, he's going to come in here and take this town apart. You just mark my words.''

''Is that a fact?'' Shelby replied. He opened the door. ''Well, then, we'd better keep you where he can find you, don't you think?''

''I'm tellin' you, old man, you're makin' a very big mistake,'' Quinn said again.

''It won't be my first mistake,'' Shelby said. He slammed the door behind them, then turned the key in the lock.

''Maybe it ain't your first. But it could be your last,'' Wilson said ominously.

''Where'd you find them?'' Shelby asked Win as he walked over to re-hang the key on the hook on the wall.

''About ten miles from here,'' Win answered. ''We found the place where they're all holed up. So, we just waited around outside long enough, and these two came out.''

''Who are they, do you know?''

''One of them is called Wilson, the other is called Quinn. That's all I know.''

''Here they are,'' Joe said. He had been leafing through a pile of wanted posters from the moment they stepped into the marshal's office. Now he pulled a couple of them out and showed them to Shelby.

''The tall one with the mustache is Cal Wilson. The short one with the beard is L. Q. Quinn.''

''I'll get word out to Doc Claymore that you brought two more in,'' Shelby said. ''Where will I find you?''

''After we take care of the horses you'll probably find us in the saloon,'' Win said.

''And if we aren't there, we'll be down to Big Kate's Place,'' Joe added.

''All right, I'll find you,'' Shelby said.

The two boys boarded their horses, as well as the two horses that belonged to the rustlers, in the livery. The sun had completely set now, and it was dark as they walked down to the bright lights of the saloon. The saloon was fairly crowded, filled with smoke and ringing with laughter and dozens of conversations. In addition to the filled tables, there were several customers standing at the bar. At a table nearest the cold stove, four men played cards.

"What'll it be?" the bartender asked.

"Beer," Joe said, answering for both of them.

The barkeep drew the beers, then put the two mugs on the bar. Joe blew some of the foam off the head, then drank his entire beer down before he lowered the mug. He set the empty stein on the bar and let out a long, satisfied sigh.

"That one was for thirst," he said. "Now I'll take one for taste."

"Be glad to," the bartender replied, refilling his mug.

Over at the card table, one of the players stood up. "Well, boys, I've enjoyed the game, but I've got to get out to the ranch. I'm ridin' night hawk."

"Nice of you to leave some of your money with us, Tim," one of the other players said, and all laughed.

"Yeah, well, I'll get it back next time." As Tim walked away, saying goodbye to the others in the saloon, he left an opening at the table.

Joe sat his mug down on the bar, empty for the second time.

"Another?" the bartender asked.

"No, thanks," Joe said. He smiled. "I've enjoyed the beer, but beer's not the only thing I come back to town for. You coming, Win?"

Win, who was looking at the table with the open chair, shook his head.

"You go ahead, Joe. I think I'll play a little cards."

Joe snorted. "I like a game of cards as much as the next fella," he said. "But I have to tell you, playing cards ain't what I've been thinkin' about these last several days out on the range."

Kelly gave a squeal of delight when she saw Joe coming through the front door. She ran to him and threw her arms around him.

"Oh, I've been wondering when you would come back," she said.

"Have you missed me?"

"Have I missed you?" She grabbed his hand, then began to pull on him as she started toward the stairs.

"What are you doing?" Joe asked.

"I'm going to show you how much I missed you," Kelly replied.

"Don't you want to visit a little?"

"We can visit later," Kelly insisted.

Kelly took Joe upstairs, then into her room. When the door was closed behind them the piano music and the laughter from the downstairs salon faded quickly into the background. The effect was sudden and dramatic. It was as if they had been magically transported to another time and place so that they were, truly, alone.

Kelly leaned over and extinguished the lantern, but the moon outside was high and so full and bright that even without the lamp, the room was still illuminated by a soft light. It cast everything in subtle shadows of silver and black, allowing them to see each other as they began to remove their clothes.

Over in the saloon, Win tried to complete a spade flush, but he drew a heart instead. With a little groan, he lay his cards down.

One of the other players chuckled. "Didn't get what you were after, eh?"

" 'Fraid not," Win said.

"Say," one of the other players said. "Did you fellas hear about what happened over to Sulphur Springs?"

"No, what happened over there? Did they catch the preacher in bed with the mayor's wife, or somethin'?"

Everyone, including Win, laughed.

"No sir. A fella named Arnold Fenton got hisself killed."

"That ain't much news," one of the other players snorted. "The way things is goin' around here, we're gettin' someone killed just about ever' day."

The man suddenly realized that he was sitting at a table with one of the men responsible for most of the killings, and he blanched, visibly, then reached for his beer to try and cover his embarrassment by taking a drink. "I . . . I'm sorry, Mr.

Coulter," he mumbled. "I didn't mean nothin' by that remark."

"That's all right, Mister," Win said easily. "My brother and I have done a lot of killing. Only thing I can say is, we haven't killed anyone who wasn't trying to kill us."

"Yeah, well, that wasn't the case with this fella over in Sulphur Springs," the first man said, trying to recapture the attention. "This fella, Fenton, was just standing there under a streetlamp. He was killed by a rifle shot from five hundred yards away. In the dark."

"What? You trying to tell us someone made a five-hundred-yard rifle shot—in the dark?"

"Yep. He was shooting one of those Whitworth rifles, you know, the kind the sharpshooters used during the war."

That bit of information got Win's attention and he looked over at the speaker.

"Did they get who did it?" he asked.

"Weren't no gettin' to it. It was all legal. Turns out the fella who did the shootin' was a bounty hunter. Fenton was a wanted man, dead or alive."

"Wanted or not, there's nothing sporting about shooting a man from concealment in the dark."

"Well, I agree with you," the storyteller said. "Still and all, you got to hand it to ole' Snell. That was one hell of a shot."

"Snell?" Win asked.

"Jarred Snell. Like I say, he's a bounty hunter. You ever run across him?"

"I damn near did," Win replied. He was convinced, now that Jarred Snell was the mysterious shooter who had killed his horse, and nearly killed him.

At that very moment, Kelly's fingers were digging into Joe's back while she lay beneath him, mindless in the throes of pleasure. She bucked beneath him as the spasms of release rippled through her flesh like wildfire. She arched her back, and Joe felt her fingernails dig deeper. Then she fell back as Joe bore into her, pulling back and holding it in exquisite agony for a long moment before plunging back into the churning hot cauldron of her sex.

They settled into an even rhythm of lovemaking, and he kissed her voluptuous breasts, making her squirm with delight. She held onto him and rocked with him, as if they were on the back of an easy-running horse. Joe stroked her gently, matching his movements to hers until shoots of pleasure coursed through his flesh, making him tingle all over.

Kelly rushed to the edge of excitement, and she urged Joe to take her to the height once more. He felt his seed boil and strain, and she sensed the urgency in him. Their strokes came faster and faster until he was no longer able to hold back, and he burst inside her, burst like a dam giving way, gushing into her like a spewing fountain.

Chapter 16

THE CARDS WEREN'T FALLING WELL, SO BIDDING GOODBYE to the other players around the table, Win quit the game. He walked on through the bar then stepped out onto the front porch for some fresh air. That was when someone came running up to him, out of breath and clearly excited about something.

"Say, aren't you one of them fellas that brought in them two rustlers today?"

"Yes."

"Iffen you don't want them to get away, you'd best get on down to the livery right away," the man said.

"Why? What's happening?"

"While the marshal was out makin' his rounds, them two prisoners got the jump on the boy that comes around ever' night to clean up the jail. Shelby seen 'em just as they was gettin' away and he's got 'em holed up in the livery. The only thing is, they killed that clean-up boy so they say they ain't got nothin' to lose now, and they ain't goin' to give up. They say they're goin' to kill the livery boy if the marshal don't let 'em go."

"Thanks," Win said. He started down the street toward the livery and saw that there were already a dozen or more people gathered around the livery stable to watch the drama unfold. He noticed, also, that none of them were offering to help the marshal. He looked around for Shelby, but didn't see him anywhere.

"Where's the marshal?" he asked one of the men in the crowd.

"He's in there," the man said, pointing to the livery barn.

"Inside?"

"Yeah. He yelled out a moment ago that he was goin' to come in after them two if they didn't come out with their hands up. When they didn't come out, why the marshal went on inside."

"That seems like a dumbfool thing to do," Win said. Despite his comment, he couldn't help but feel that his earlier scorn for the marshal may have been misplaced.

Win would like to have had Joe with him. The two brothers worked so well as a team that they didn't even have to speak . . . each of them knew, instinctively, what the other would do. But Joe wasn't here and there was no time to wait for him. If he didn't act quickly, the marshal, and perhaps the stable boy, might be killed.

Pulling his pistol, he started toward the livery. He was almost there when he heard a muffled gunshot from the dark. He broke out into a run and had just reached the edge of the livery when he saw Shelby coming out of the shadows toward him.

"Shelby? Shelby, what is it? What's going on?" Win called. "I heard a shot."

"I'm killed, Coulter," Shelby said with a half smile on his face. He fell face down to the ground and Win ran over to him then rolled him over.

"Marshal?" Win called, but there was no answer. Shelby was right. He had been killed.

"There goes one of 'em, Coulter!" a man suddenly shouted from the other side of the livery. Win drew his pistol and stared out into the empty darkness.

A figure suddenly appeared near the corner of the livery barn. He was tall and lanky and in the ambient light, Win could see the walrus-type mustache. This was Wilson.

"Give it up, Wilson!" Win called.

In answer, Wilson pointed his pistol toward Win and it

boomed three times. In the light of the muzzle-flash, Win could see the wild, desperate features of his face.

Win shot back, only once, but once was enough. His bullet found its mark and Wilson threw up his gun and fell over backward. Win ran over to the fallen outlaw and knelt beside him. He could see bubbles of blood coming from Wilson's mouth. He was trying hard to breathe, and Win heard a sucking sound in his chest. He knew that his bullet had punctured Wilson's lungs.

"Why didn't you give it up when I called to you?" Win asked.

"I figure this beats hangin'," Wilson gasped.

"What about it, Mister? Is he dead?" someone asked from behind Win.

"He soon will be," Win answered. He saw the townspeople beginning to stream across the street, drawn by morbid curiosity, anxious to get a look at the bodies of Marshal Shelby and Cal Wilson.

"Look at that," someone said, pointing to Wilson. "He got him dead center with one shot."

Frustrated by the gathering crowd, Win stood up and waved at them. "Listen to me. You folks better get back if you don't want to get shot," he called. "There's still one left in the barn."

Almost as if in punctuation to Win's statement, there was a flash of light, then the crash of gunfire as someone fired from inside the livery. Though the bullet didn't hit anyone, it whistled so close over the heads of those in the crowd that it had the effect that Win's warning did not. With a little shout of fear, everyone turned and ran to get out of the way of the line of fire.

"He's still in there!" someone said, repeating Win's warning.

"The damned fool tried to shoot us," another said. The crowd, still unwilling to miss the show, stayed in close proximity. Now, however, they prudently found shelter behind the corners of adjacent buildings, or behind the nearby watering troughs.

"Quinn! Quinn, give it up," Win called into the livery.

"Now why would I want to do that?" Quinn called back.

"Because there's only one of two ways you are going to come out of there. Either with your hands up, or dead."

"I ain't givin' up."

"Then you're coming out dead," Win warned.

"I don't think so. I've got an edge, Coulter."

"You've got nothing."

"I've got the stable boy," Quinn called. He giggled.

"So what?"

"So what? If you try and come in here, I'm goin' to kill him, that's so what." Quinn giggled again, confident of his bargaining position.

"Hell, that boy doesn't mean anything to me. Go ahead and kill him," Win called back. He could hear the townspeople gasping around him.

"What? What do you mean kill him?"

"I mean just what I said," Win replied. "Kill him and get it over with. Then there will just be the two of us."

"You're runnin' a bluff. You think I won't kill him?"

"Look, kill him or don't kill him," Win said. "I don't care which you do. Just shut up about it."

"You're . . . you're crazy. You know that?"

"Maybe," Win said. "But I'm not the one trapped in a livery."

"Is Wilson dead?"

"Yes."

"It was him killed the marshal. Not me," Quinn said. "All I wanted to do was to get out of here."

"Is the stable boy still alive?" Win asked.

"Yes."

"Can he testify that Wilson is the one who shot the marshal?"

"Yeah, he seen it."

"Send him out."

"No. He's the only chance I have. If I come out, he's going to be standing in front of me."

"Look, I'll make this easy for both of us. Have the stable boy stand in the door and I'll kill him myself. We can just get him out of the way now," Win said.

"No, wait, wait!" Quinn called. "Maybe we can make a deal."

"What kind of deal?"

"I don't want to hang. I didn't kill the marshal."

"Well, you could always let the stable boy go. That way he could testify, and it might make you look good for the jury."

"All right," Quinn called from the darkened interior. "All right, I'm comin' out now. I'm sending the stable boy out first. Don't shoot him."

"Go ahead."

The door to the livery opened and the stable boy stuck his head out, tentatively, then ran from the barn.

"He's out," Win said. "Now it's your turn."

"Don't shoot."

"Come out with your hands up," Win said. "I won't shoot."

Quinn, like the stable boy before him, stuck his head around the edge of the door and searched anxiously up and down the street. He tossed his pistol out into the dirt.

"There," he called. "I ain't armed."

"Get your hands up and come on out."

Quinn stepped outside. Then, with his hands in the air, he started toward Win. He took only three steps when, from one of the darkened buildings back in the town, a rifle barked. Quinn crumpled and went down.

"Who fired that shot?" Win yelled over his shoulder. "Who fired?"

No one answered and Win hurried over to Quinn's crumpled body.

"I thought you wouldn't shoot," Quinn coughed.

"I didn't," Win answered. "I don't know who did it."

Quinn tried to laugh, but a spasm of coughing overtook him instead. "Why did he shoot me?" he asked. "I wasn't goin' to say anything."

"Why did who shoot you?"

Quinn's breath came in a series of raspy gasps.

"Quinn, who do you think shot you?"

The raspy gasps stopped and Win put his hand to Quinn's neck. He was dead.

Once again the townspeople began to press forward. This time there was no one remaining to threaten their safety so that, within a few moments, the crowd around the three bodies had grown quite large.

"Well, Mr. Coulter," Doc Claymore said. "I got word from Marshal Shelby that you had brought in two live rustlers. Only by the time I got here, I learned that he was mistaken. Your prisoners are dead, and so is the marshal."

"Yeah," Win said.

"Death does seem to follow you, doesn't it?"

"I reckon it does."

Claymore sighed. "Well, there's no sense in belaboring the issue any longer. I have twice brought it to a vote to have you dismissed, and I have been defeated both times. If the Association wants to keep you on, to include your rather severe brand of justice, then I feel it is no longer my place to challenge you. Stop by tomorrow morning at seven o'clock. I'll have your money ready for you."

"Say, Mister," the stable boy said, coming up to Win. "Would you really have killed me to get at him?" He nodded toward Quinn's body.

"Did you believe that?" Win asked.

"You're damned right I believed it," the stable boy replied.

"Then Quinn probably believed it too," Win said. "It took away his edge."

"But would you really have done it?"

Win smiled. "If I told you, it would take away my edge," he said.

"Damn!" Potter said when he heard the news of what happened to Wilson and Quinn. "The Coulters again. I'm tellin' you, if we don't get rid of them, they're going to get rid of us."

"Yeah, well, it ain't like we haven't been trying. They take a lot of killin', that's all."

"Bullshit. They don't take no more killin' than anyone

else," Potter said. "We just got to be a little smarter with it, that's all."

When Win and Joe dropped by the office of the Cattlemen's Association at seven the next morning, they learned that, once more, Doc Claymore had called a special meeting. Several of the ranchers' horses were already tied up at the hitching rail, a couple of buggies were parked on the street, and Vogel and Baker were just arriving.

"I heard about the little fracas last night," Baker said. "Congratulations on doin' a good job."

"Thanks," Win said. He took in all the other horses with a sweep of his hand. "What's going on? Is there a meeting this morning?"

"Yes," Baker answered. "After Shelby got himself killed last night, Doc Claymore sent word out to all of us, asking us to be here at seven this morning. You mean you don't know anything about it?"

"No," Win answered.

"Say, where is Truelove?" Vogel asked.

"I imagine he'll be along," Baker said. Baker chuckled. "Until this meeting was called, there were several of us going to go over there and help him finish roofing his house, remember?"

"Yeah," Vogel laughed. "I don't reckon he'll want to tackle that job with just him and Ev."

The other ranchers were already sitting around the meeting table when Win, Baker, and Vogel went inside. Claymore was at the head of the table and, with an expansive gesture, he invited them to sit down.

"Gentlemen, what do you say we get the meeting started?" Claymore began.

"Wait a minute. What about Truelove? He ain't here yet."

"Truelove won't be here, I'm afraid. He sent word that he wasn't going to be able to come. He has to run over to Sweetwater today." Claymore held up a piece of paper. "However, he gave me authorization to vote his proxy, if nobody protests."

"That's all right by me," Vogel said. "What about the rest of you?"

"I got no problems," one of the others said. "Baker?"

"I guess it's all right. But what's this meeting about, anyway?"

"A couple of things," Claymore said. He looked over at the Coulters. "To begin with, Mr. Coulter, Mr. Coulter, I've been pretty hard on the two of you, lately, and I want to apologize," he said. "Several of the good people of this town have told me what happened last night and, under the circumstances, there was nothing else you could do." He slid an envelope across the table toward him. "Your money is in this envelope and I want to go on record here and now, as saying that you have my complete confidence. In fact, I would like to show that confidence by offering you a position. As you know, we are now in need of a town marshal. I'm prepared to offer the job of marshal and deputy marshal to the two of you."

"Thanks for the offer," Win said, taking the envelope. "But we aren't interested."

Claymore nodded. "I didn't really think you would be. Nor should you be, actually. The truth is, you are much more effective the way you are. However, I thought it only right that the position be offered to the two of you, or, either of you for that matter, before we offered it to anyone else." He looked at the others around the table. "However, gentlemen, his refusal does leave us with a problem. We have to have a new marshal and I'm asking for any suggestions."

"What about you, Doc?" one of the other ranchers proposed.

"Me? No, I don't see myself as marshal."

"Wait a minute, why not?" Baker asked. "You're the head of the Cattlemen's Association. You could combine the two jobs."

"Gentlemen, you forget I have a ranch to run. A larger ranch, I might add, than any of you."

"Well, yes, but you've found the time to be president of the Cattlemen's Association. You can find time to do this as well. It needs doin', Doc, you can't get around that."

"But being a marshal is a full-time job."

"It don't have to be. I mean, you've got a foreman to help with the ranch, and you can appoint as many deputies as you want to help with the marshaling," one of the other men said. "Come on, Doc, we're not sayin' you have to make night rounds like Shelby did. Just sort of be over things."

"Like a general," another suggested.

"A general," Claymore said. He smiled. "Well, as someone who never got any higher than private in the war, I must confess that I like the sound of that." He drummed his fingers on the table for a while, then he nodded his head. "All right," he said. "I am committed to running the rustlers out and bringing peace to the valley. And if the only way to do that is to be your marshal, then I'll be your marshal. But only until this business is all taken care of. After that, like a general after a war is over, I intend to go back to being a private citizen and a rancher. I hope, a prosperous rancher."

The others laughed, then there was a spattering of applause around the table. Claymore looked over at Win and Joe.

"Gentlemen, now that I am officially the marshal I'll say the same thing I said a few moments ago as a rancher and as the head of the Cattlemen's Association. I appreciate, that is, we all appreciate the job you've been doing and you have my full and complete support."

"Thanks," Win said again. He and Joe stood up. "Now, if you men will excuse us, we're going to get a little breakfast, then go back to work."

"Good luck," Claymore called to them. "Now, gentlemen, I want to talk about the price per head at the cattle pens in Kansas City. I think we can . . ." That was as far as Claymore got before Win and Joe left the office. Then they walked across the street to the Alhambra Cafe.

Although Joe, of the two brothers, was known as the biggest eater, on this morning Win more than held his own. Breakfast consisted of a stack of pancakes, two eggs, fried potatoes, an oversized piece of ham, and half a dozen biscuits each. They were just washing it all down with a second cup of coffee when an old Mexican woman came into the cafe, looked around until she saw them, then shuffled over to their table.

"You are the Señors Coulter?" she asked.

"Yes."

"This is for you." She handed him a note.

Coulter,

We have the Truelove girl.

Potter

"Wait!" Win called, standing up quickly. The woman stopped. "Where did you get this?"

"A man gave it to me," she answered. "He gave me money to give it to you."

"What man?" Win asked. He had given the note to Joe who, by now, had read it as well.

"I do not know him, Señor. I do laundry at the edge of town. He rode in, gave me the note, then rode away."

"Thanks," Win said. He took the note back from Joe and looked at it again, then, with a sigh of frustration, put it in his pocket.

"We've got to go after her," Win said.

"You'll get no argument from me, Big Brother," Joe said. "But you know what you always say."

"Yeah, I know. But we're going after her," Win said again.

Win knew what Joe was talking about. They were now faced with the very situation they were always trying to avoid. Because of the kind of life they led, they made it a practice never to establish relationships with anyone, male or female. This wasn't because of any particular antisocial behavior on their part, this was based upon a very sound principle. They knew they could always be responsible for themselves, but they couldn't always be responsible for anyone else. That wasn't a very healthy situation, for if they were close to anyone, an enemy could get to them through that person. On the other hand if they were close to no one, an enemy would have no way to get to them. In this way they were able to deny any potential enemy an "edge."

For the most part, the theory worked well. Sometimes, however, there were those borderline cases where one or both of them might be vulnerable. Lucy Truelove was just such a case. Though no official relationship had been established between Win and Lucy Truelove, their paths had crossed frequently enough that Win could no longer regard her with total detachment. Even the horse he was riding now had been a gift from Lucy Truelove and her father. If Potter did have her, Win knew that he had no choice. He would have to go after her.

Potter had found his edge. Win didn't like it much when the other fellow had an edge.

Chapter 17

AT FIRST IT WAS JUST A THIN WISP, LIKE NOTHING MORE THAN a column of dust in the distance. But as the Coulters drew closer to the Truelove Ranch, the wisp of dust took on more substance until it became a column of smoke, growing thicker and heavier until finally it was a heavy, black cloud, filled with glowing embers and roiling into the sky.

This was Potter's second visit to the ranch and, like before, he had left fire and smoke as his calling cards. Once again, Potter was burning them out.

The fire was still snapping and popping when Win and Joe arrived but there was little left to burn. The new house, so recently built to replace the one that had been burned out before, was now a twisted mass of blackened timbers with just enough fuel left to support the dying flames.

Potter had been more thorough this time than he had been before, because this time the barn, smokehouse, and grainery were also in flames. In addition to the fires there had been a wanton slaughter of all the farm animals. Two dray-horses lay dead in the corral, half a dozen pigs were slaughtered, and there were even a handful of dead chickens scattered about.

Win saw Truelove then, facedown in a pool of his own blood. When he went over to get a closer look at the rancher, he saw that the older man had been shot several times in the head and chest. He knew, even before he reached him, that

Truelove was dead. Martha, also dead, was lying nearby, at his side in death as she had been in life.

"Coulter? Coulter, is that you?" The voice that called was strained with pain and when Win looked toward it, he saw Ev on the ground over near the watering trough. He hurried over to him. "We sure could've used your gun this time, partner," Ev said.

"When did this happen?" Win asked.

"This mornin', just after daylight," Ev answered. "We sure wasn't expectin' nothin' like this. They wasn't after to steal nothin'. They just come out here to murder and to burn. They went plumb crazy. After they shot me an' Mr. and Mrs. True-love, they commenced to killin' all the animals. No reason for it, they didn't take no meat nor nothin', they just killed and killed and killed. By then there wasn't nothin' left I could do, so I just lay over here real still and pretended to be dead." He sat up and Win saw that he had at least three bullet holes in him, two in the thigh and one in the arm. They were painful and he had lost a lot of blood, but he would probably live.

"Who did this, Ev? Was it Potter?"

"Yeah, it was Potter. Him and about eight others," Ev said. "I got two of 'em. You'll find 'em over there, both dead. But there's at least six, maybe seven of 'em left."

"You did all you could do," Win said.

Suddenly Ev reached up and grabbed Win's arm and sqee-zed it tight, as if just remembering something that was important. "They got Lucy, Coulter. They got Lucy and they took her off with them. She was callin' for me to help her but I . . . I couldn't do nothin' for her. Go after her, Coulter. Get her back from those bastards."

"They're using her as bait," Win said. "They took her to get us to come after them."

"Well, hell, you are goin' after her, ain't you?"

"I don't know," Win said. "I do know that that is what they want us to do."

Ev raised his gun and pointed it at Win, though he had such little strength to keep it up, that the barrel weaved around in tiny circles.

"Damnit, man," Ev said. "Didn't you hear what I said?

They got Lucy! Now, tell me you're going to bring her back safe, or so help me God I'll shoot you myself.''

"Is that what you want to do, Ev?" Win asked, easily.

Ev lowered the gun and shook his head.

"Don't worry, we're going after her," Win said easily. "And we'll bring her back, I promise."

"I'm goin' to hold you to that, Coulter," Ev said. "I can't go myself, so you two boys are the only chance she's got."

"We'll get her," Win promised, hating the fact that he had let himself get so involved, yet determined to follow through with his promise.

"Thanks," Ev said. He smiled broadly. "I knew I could count on you boys." He held his gun up and looked at it, then smiled. "Couldn't of shot you anyway," he said. "I already used up all the bullets. That's why I had to just lie here an' watch helplessly."

"Which way did they go, Ev?" Joe asked.

"North."

"North?" That surprised Win. He and Joe had located the hideout, and it was south of the ranch. However, they might have known by now that they had been found. If so, they would have to go someplace else.

"Coulter. Lucy's wearin' a red dress. You ought to be able to spot that a mile away."

"Thanks."

"Bring her back to me, Coulter. There's somethin' I ain't ever got aroun' to tellin' her yet."

Lucy sat on her horse looking at Potter and the others who had come to kill her ma and pa and Ev, then burn her ranch. Potter was holding his hat in his hand, wiping his hairless brow with a bandanna. He looked back at Lucy and laughed a greasy, evil-sounding laugh.

"How are you doin' little lady? Are you holdin' up all right?"

"I find it hard to believe that you are actually concerned about my comfort," Lucy replied sarcastically.

"Yeah, sure," Potter said. "After all, I want to be a good host." He laughed at his own joke.

"Why did you kill all the others but take me?"

"Why do you care? You're alive, ain't you? Ain't that all that's important?"

"No. There are some things that are more important than merely being alive."

"Yeah? Well, maybe for folks like you, folks who are noble and all that. But I ain't noble. Tell me about the Coulters."

"What?" Lucy asked, surprised by the question.

"Win and Joe Coulter. The fellas they call the Bushwhackers. Tell me about them."

"What do you want to know? They're good men."

"Will they come for you?"

"Will they come for me? I don't know. Why should they come for me?"

"Because I sent them a note tellin' them I had you," Potter said.

Lucy looked surprised. "You told them where I was? Why would you do that?"

"Don't you understand anything at all? I'm usin' you, girlie. I'm usin' you as bait."

Potter pulled his pistol and turned the cylinder to check the loads, then he put the pistol back in his holster.

"You did all this just to get the Coulters to come after you?" Lucy asked. "You're mad! They have been after you all along. That's the whole reason they're here."

"Yeah, well, I want them on my own terms," Potter said. "From what I hear, they aren't the kind of men you mess with. I've always heard that Win Coulter was the fastest one with a gun . . . but nobody ever' told me how fast Joe was. I hear that when he gunned down Harley Claymore, he was fast as greased lightnin'." Potter pulled his lips tight across his teeth in what might have been a smile. "That must mean Win is even faster'n greased lightnin'."

"If they are as good as all that, why would you even want them coming after you?" Lucy asked. "Aren't you afraid they might kill you?"

"I figure on tippin' the odds in my favor a bit," Potter said. "Then, afer I kill them, I'll be known all over as the man who got the Bushwhackers."

Ahead of Win and Joe, the brown land lay in empty folds of rocks, dirt and cactus. The sun heated the ground then sent up undulating waves which caused near objects to shimmer, and nonexistent lakes to appear tantalizingly in the distance. Joe picked up the tracks, but the ground was hard and the signs so indistinct that he couldn't tell very much about them. He didn't know if Lucy was one of the riders or not.

"You're the tracker, Little Brother," Win said. "What do you think?"

"All I can do is go with what my gut tells me," Joe said. "And my gut tells me we're on the right track."

Half an hour later, Joe's gut instinct was proven correct when a rifle bullet fried the air between them.

"Win!"

"I'm all right!" Win answered. "Where is he? Do you see him?"

"No!"

Both brothers dismounted, then slapped the flanks of their horses to send them out of danger. As they dived behind a nearby rock outcropping, the would-be assailant fired again. The bullet ricocheted off a rock very near Win, sending shreds of hot lead into his face before it whined away from him.

The hidden gunman laughed. "Pretty close, wasn't I? Did that sting a little?"

"Where's the girl?" Win called.

"The girl? She's with Potter and the others," the voice answered.

"They leave you behind for the dirty work?"

"No. I volunteered to stay behind. You see, we've got us a pretty good pot built up for whoever kills you. I reckon that's goin' to be me."

"I doubt it. You've already missed your chance."

"They say both you boys are pretty good," the gunmen called. "How good are you?"

"Good enough to stay alive," Win called back. He motioned to Joe to move to another position so they wouldn't be bunched together and, nodding, Joe complied.

"Well I don't think just being good counts for much. I think the only thing that counts is a measure of guts. And I got that. The name's Mayhan. Eddie Mayhan. You ever heard of me?''

"Can't say as I have," Win answered.

"Yeah? Well, after I kill both of you, I reckon folks will know who I am.''

"You aren't afraid of us, Mayhan?''

"Naw, I ain't afraid. The way I've heard it, you two boys do most of your shootin' in the back, or against blowhards like Harley Claymore. He was a blowhard, you know.''

"I'd say you called it about right," Win replied. "Harley Claymore was pretty much of a blowhard.'' He moved around, trying to get into position to see his assailant.

"Say, Coulter, how'd you like it if we was to both put our guns in our holsters then step out into the open, just to see how things would come out?''

"There are two of us. Which one of us do you want?''

"I don't care which one of you I face, as long as the other one stands up in plain sight. I don't want to be shot in the back.''

"Are you that brave?'' Win asked.

"Well, I sure ain't goin' to piss in my pants just 'cause you say boo. I believe I can take either one of you. What do you say we try it?''

Win looked around the rock and saw that Mayhan was coming from behind his cover with his pistol holstered and his hands spread out beside him.

"Come on, Mr. Coulter. I'm already out here.''

Win nodded at Joe, who, by now, had nearly flanked the gunman's position, and both of them stood up. The gunman seemed surprised to see that Win and Joe had managed to get that much separation between them.

Win and Joe both holstered their pistols. "I didn't really think you'd do it.''

"Well, I'm a surprising man," Mayhan said with an evil grin. "Now!'' he suddenly shouted.

Two shots went off, one from Win's immediate right, and another from behind the rock where Mayhan had been. One shot was aimed for Win, the other for Joe. Both bullets missed, though Win didn't know how the one that was aimed at him

ould have, because he was so close to the shooter that he felt
he sting of burnt gunpowder.

"You dumb bastards! You missed! Both of you!" Mayhan
houted as he went for his own gun.

Win had a fifth of a second to make a decision. Should he
ire at Eddie Mayhan who was just now going for his gun, or
hould he shoot at gunman who was now rising up from be-
ind a nearby rock with his gun already in his hand?

Joe had no such decision to make. He picked out the one
vho shot at him, and was returning fire. Win decided to take
n Mayhan. The gunman nearest him had already demon-
trated his poor marksmanship in the missed shot, whereas
Mayhan had come much closer on his first shot.

Even as he was thinking about it, Win's gun was cocked
nd booming. The bullet slammed into Mayhan's chest, sev-
ring arteries and tearing away heart tissue. Mayhan was dead
efore he hit the ground, and even before he fell, Win was
lready turning to fire at the other gunman. The gunman's
econd shot proved as ineffective as his first, but Win's bullet
it the man in the hip, causing him to double over, then crum-
le down in pain.

At the same time, another body came sliding, head-down,
rom the rocks, the victim of Joe's well placed shot.

The sound of the shooting echoed and re-echoed, as if the
ghosts of the men Win and Joe had just killed were continuing
he battle. When the last echo was a subdued rumble off a
listant hill, the silence of the desert returned. The limbs of a
earby ocotillo rattled dryly in the breeze. A shock of tum-
leweed bounced by. A lizard scurried across a rock.

"Oh," the wounded gunman moaned. "Oh, shit, it hurts. I
in't never had nothin' to hurt like this."

"Are there any others around?" Win asked. Neither he nor
oe had holstered their pistols. Both men were looking toward
he rocks and crevices for any sign of yet another hidden as-
ailant.

"No, there was just the three of us," the gunman said
hrough teeth, clenched in pain. "Mayhan said it would be
asy."

"Nothing is easy," Win said, putting his gun away. "Where is the Truelove girl?"

"I'm gutshot," the gunman said.

Joe knelt beside him, and looked at the bullet hole. It was in the hip, painful, but not fatal.

"My brother must be losing his touch. You aren't gutshot," Joe said.

"I'm goin' to die."

"No you won't. Not unless I kill you," Win said. "And I will, if you don't tell me where Potter and the girl are."

"I can't tell you that. Potter will kill me if I tell you."

"I'll kill you if you don't."

The wounded gunman shook his head no.

"If that's the way you want it," Win said easily. He pointed his pistol at the wounded gunman's head.

"Wait, Win, you got to kill the last one who didn't talk," Joe said. "Let me kill this one."

"All right, Little Brother, be my guest," Win invited.

Joe cocked his pistol. The cylinder turned with a metallic click, lining up the next cartridge under the hammer and firing pin. The knuckle of his trigger finger whitened.

"No!" the gunman screamed, covering his head with his arms. "No, don't kill me!"

"Where's the girl?" Win asked again.

"This ambush wasn't my idea," the gunman said. "It wasn't even Mayhan's. It was Potter's. He told Mayhan he'd double the pot if him and me and Jones would stay back and take care of you."

"One last time. Where is the girl?"

"All I know is they were headed for a little Mex town called Mezquita."

"Give me your gun," Win said.

"What?"

"I said give me your gun."

"Look here, Coulter. You ain't goin' to leave me out here unarmed, are you? They might be Indians around. Snakes, wolves, all sorts of things."

"We're doin' you a favor," Win said. "The way you shoot, you're likely to shoot yourself."

Win took the gun from Mayhan's hand. Joe went over to the other gunman's body, and took his gun as well.

"Where are your horses?"

"Right over there, behind them rocks," the wounded gunman answered, pointing off to his left.

Win walked over and retrieved the three horses. He shoved the pistols into the saddle bag of one of the animals.

"Take off your boots," Win ordered.

The gunman did as he was instructed and Win put the boots in the stirrups, then slapped the horses on the flanks, sending them running.

"Wait a minute! You're leavin' me out here with no gun, no horse, no water, and no boots," Arnie complained. "You can't do that! I'll die!"

"There's a town about six miles that way," Win said, pointing off to the southeast. "If you start now, you can make it there. If you try to go anywhere else, you will die. You better get goin'. The longer you stay out here, the thirstier you're goin' to get."

"I'll get you for this, Coulter," the wounded gunman said. "I'll get both of you. One of these days I'll run across you two again, and when I do, I'll get you."

"Yeah, keep thinking about that," Win suggested. "It'll keep you going."

The wounded gunman started toward the southwest, his progress impeded not only by his lack of boots, but also by the fact that he was carrying a bullet in his hip. Win watched until Joe came back with their horses. Then the two brothers swung into the saddle and rode west, heading toward Mezquita.

Chapter 18

MEZQUITA WAS NO DIFFERENT FROM ANY OF THE OTHER Mexican towns scattered throughout the American Southwest. The Mexican flavor dictated its layout . . . a dozen or more adobe buildings scattered around a large square. This village did happen to have a church though, a large mission which stood guard at the east end of town. The shadow of the cross fell across the churchyard as Win and Joe rode up. The padre was drawing water from a well and the two brothers dismounted and walked toward him. The priest wore a brown cassock, held together with a strip of black rawhide, from which dangled an oversized wooden crucifix. A bald spot shined from the top of the priest's head. The hair around the bald spot was gray.

"Padre," Win said, nodding at the priest.

The priest nodded back, studying the two men closely.

"We'd be obliged for a drink," Win said. "The water in our canteens has grown a little stale." Win pulled out a couple of bills and handed them to the priest.

"This is God's water," the priest said, waving the money away. "It's free."

"The money isn't for His water, it's for His church," Win said, nodding toward the building.

The priest smiled. "*Si, gracias.* Bless you, my sons, bless you," he said, taking the money.

Win plunged the dipper into the bucket and scooped up the

water, then drank long and deep. Joe didn't wait for the dipper, but just turned the bucket up and drank from it. The water was cool and delicious, and they drank until their bellies were full.

"Would you like to fill your canteens?" the priest offered.

"Yes, thank you," Joe said. He walked over to the horses and got both his and Win's canteens, poured out the old water, then began refilling them with fresh water, pouring it from the dipper.

"Padre, we're looking for some men who may have come in here. I'm not sure how many. Four or five of them, I would guess. And one girl. The girl with them would be young and pretty. Also, she would be wearing a red dress."

"There are five men," the priest replied. "Are they friends of yours?"

"No, I wouldn't call them friends."

"I did not think so," the priest replied. The priest studied Win and Joe for a long moment. Win felt strange, as if the priest's eyes could penetrate to his very soul. Under the priest's gaze he was stripped naked with all his past sins, actual and conceived, bared. "I am confused," the priest finally said.

"What has you confused?"

"You two have come to kill these men. This I know, for there is death in the eyes of both of you. I see also, that you are men who have killed many times, but I do not see pleasure in the killing."

"Padre, the men we seek are very evil," Win said. "They have killed many times, and they *do* kill for pleasure. They killed the girl's mother and father, and all those who worked on the girl's ranch."

"If I tell you and you kill them, I will be a party to it," the priest said. "I do not wish to help you kill the men."

"I think when they are through with the girl, they will kill her. If you do not wish to help us kill these men, then consider that you are helping us save the girl."

"Si. Si, I will help the girl," the padre said. "Very well, the men you are seeking, five men and a girl, rode into town early today. Then, a bit later, four men and the girl rode out."

"Only four rode out? Then that means one of the men is still here?"

"*Si.*"

"What does he look like?"

"This I cannot tell you," the priest said. "I did not see any of them closely."

"Thank you," Win said. "You have been a big help."

"I will pray for the safety of the girl, Señor," the priest said.

Joe took the horses to the stable, not to board them, but to see to it that they were fed and watered. If the chase was to continue, their horses would have to be refreshed. As Joe led the horses into the stable, he saw his brother crossing the street, heading for the cantina.

The entrance to the cantina was protected, not by bat-wing doors as was routine in the more Americanized towns, but by several strings of beads. Win stood on the porch just outside the cantina for a long moment, just listening to the sounds from inside. Someone was strumming a guitar, but that didn't stop the flow of conversation. The words were Spanish mostly, though he heard a few English-speaking voices. The beads clacked against each other as Win pushed through.

Pulling his hat brim low, he stepped up to the end of the bar then looked through the place. There were more than three dozen men and women in here. Several were standing at the bar, many others were sitting around the tables. One Mexican was in a chair against the wall, holding a pretty girl, obviously one of the bar-girls, on his lap.

There were only four Americans in the bar. Figuring that his man had to be one of the four, he studied them closely. Even as he studied them though, he realized that the cantina had a few rooms in the back to be used by the whores, or *putas*, as the Mexicans called the women of the trade. It was possible that his man could be back there. He slapped the bar.

"*Si?*" the bartender asked, sliding down the bar to stand before him.

"Beer."

"We have only tequila."

"All right, tequila," Win said, putting his coin on the bar.

The bartender filled a glass and Win took a drink, screwing his face up against its controlled fire.

One of the Americans laughed. "What's the matter, Mister? You don't like Mexican Mule Piss?" he asked. The others laughed with him.

"Sure," Win answered. "I like it just fine."

"Say, why don't you come over here and join us in a friendly game of cards?" one of the other cowboys called. "We don't get too many Americans through here."

"Yeah," the first one said. "There's just the four of us and we get tired of looking at each other's ugly mugs every day."

Win took his drink over to the table and sat down to join them. "You mean all four of you live here."

"Yeah. I'm Slim, that's Beans, he's Poke and that's Dusty. We cowboy for Señor Soltano. Ain't that somethin' though? I mean a bunch of American's workin' for a Mexican."

"Soltano is Mex, all right, but he's fair and he pays good wages," Beans said.

"Yeah," Slim agreed. "He's a good man. Don't get us wrong, we ain't apologizin' for workin' for him or nothin'. Just remarkin' on it, that's all."

Win studied the men closely and realized that they were telling the truth. They had the look of cowboys, in their faces and in their eyes. Also, their hands were callused from hard work. These weren't outlaws.

"Are there rooms back there?" Win asked, pointing toward the rear of the building.

"Yeah," Slim answered, laughing. "You wantin' to go back there?"

"If you do, ask ole' Dusty here which one of these girls is best. He knows 'em all," Poke teased, and the others laughed at Dusty's expense.

"Anyone back there now?" Win asked. "Americans, I mean?"

"Ain't no other Americans here a'tall, 'cept just what's sittin' around this table," Slim said.

"Why do you ask?" Poke inquired.

"No reason in particular," Win answered. "I stopped down

at the church to fill my canteen and the padre said five American men and one girl rode in today. I was just curious about them.''

"Yeah, well, a group of them rode in today, but they didn't stay.''

"No, they come in and bought a bottle then went right on. Weren't very friendly.''

"Anyhow, they wasn't all Americans," Slim said.

"What?''

"They wasn't all Americans," Slim insisted. "Four of them was, and I think the girl was, but she stayed outside on her horse and didn't come in so I never got a good look at her.''

"What color dress was she wearing?''

"It was red," Poke said. "You fellas remember that 'cause Dusty said they weren't nothin' no prettier than a woman in a red dress.''

"I thought you didn't get a good look at her," Win said.

Slim laughed. "Dusty don't have to get a good look. To him all women is pretty, whether they be wearin' a red dress or not.''

"The other man was Mex," Dusty said. "And he didn't ride out with the others, neither. Leastwise, I don't remember seein' him leave.''

Win had no idea what made him look around at that precise moment. Maybe it was the fact that he had just learned that one of the men he was looking for was Mexican and he decided to look again at those in the bar. Or maybe he heard something. Or, maybe it was true, what they sometimes said of gunfighters, that they had a sixth sense about danger. For whatever reason, Win looked around, just as the Mexican against the wall was dumping the bargirl from his lap. She screamed in surprise and fright as the Mexican came up with a pistol in his hand.

"What the hell?" Slim asked. "You fellas look out!" He and the other cowboys dived for the floor, just as the Mexican fired.

Win brought his own gun up, even as the Mexican's gun burst the firing cap. The Mexican's bullet hit the deck of cards the cowboys had been playing with, sending them scattering.

The cowboys weren't the only ones on the floor. By now everyone else in the place had also dived for cover, leaving only Win and the Mexican standing. But the Mexican didn't stand for long because Win fired before the Mexican could pull the trigger a second time.

The heavy slug from Win's gun sent the Mexican crashing through a nearby table. Glasses and bottles tumbled and tequila spilled to merge with the blood which was already begininng to pool on the floor. The gunsmoke drifted slowly up to the ceiling, then spread out in a wide, nostril-burning cloud. Win looked around the room quickly to see if anyone else might represent danger, but he saw only the faces of the customers and they showed only fear, awe, and surprise.

"Damn!" Dusty said into the silence that followed the two gunshots.

"Was he the one with the Americans?" Win asked.

Poke repeated the question in Spanish, and half a dozen of the Mexican customers nodded in the affirmative.

"Yeah, he was," Poke said.

"Is he dead?"

Again the question was repeated in Spanish, and one of those who had hurried over to look at him, now nodded yes. "*Si, Señor*. He is dead."

"Damn. I didn't want to kill him," Win said. "I needed some information from him."

"You didn't want to kill him, huh?" Slim asked. He chuckled. "Well, you shot pretty straight for someone who didn't want him dead."

It was very late in the afternoon when Joe saw some horse droppings that told him they were gaining on Potter and the others.

Thirty minutes later, they came across a pass in the rocks that was so narrow they could only ride in single file. As Joe was tracking, he went through the draw first. Just as he emerged on the other side, he was shot from ambush. He had not heard nor suspected anything until the moment the bullet hit him, a sudden, numbing, sledge-hammer blow to his arm that knocked him from his horse. Immediately after that, a man jumped out from behind a rock and charged after him, firing his pistol as he ran. The bullets hit the ground around him, riccochetted off the rocks, then sailed off, filling the canyon with their angry whine.

Joe had been hit in his left arm and that caused him to fall on his right side. He was lying on his right side and thus unable to get to his gun. Incredibly, that opportunity was all the assailant saw, and he closed to within three feet of Joe, so intent on finishing him off that he didn't even notice Win, who was just coming out of the draw.

"I've got you, Coulter! I've got you!" Cain yelled excitedly, pointing his pistol at Joe's head.

Win didn't have time to shout a warning. All he had time for was to pull the trigger. His bullet tore into the attacker's throat. Cain gagged, dropped his gun, and put both hands to his neck. Win shot again and this time his bullet hit him right in the middle of the face, tearing away his nose.

"Win!" Joe shouted. By now Joe had his own gun out and he fired, even as he shouted. His bullet found its mark, and a second ambusher fell, his gun clattering down across the rocks before him.

As the man slid down, head first, Win looked around for more. He heard a horse riding away and he climbed, quickly, up onto the same rock from which the last man had been killed, to see if he could get a shot at the one who was running. It was too late. Whoever it was got away.

Win came back down from the rock, as Joe was looking at the two dead men.

"This is our old friend, Cain," Joe said, pointing to the man with his nose shot away.

"He looks bad," Win said.

"Yeah," Joe agreed. "But, you have to admit, he never was all that good looking when he was alive." Joe took the bandanna from around his neck and began trying to tie it around his wound.

"Here, let me do that," Win said, finishing the task. He tightened the bandanna.

"Damn, don't be so rough. You're squeezing my arm in two," Joe complained.

"Have to," Win replied. "Otherwise you could bleed to death."

"That might be preferable to letting you doctor me," Joe teased.

Chapter 19

LUCY AND HER CAPTORS HAD REACHED THE OLD, DESERTED
line cabin earlier that afternoon. Now Lucy lay on a filthy cot,
her hands tied to what was left of the headboard and her feet
tied to the broken footrail.

During the long afternoon, she had watched the dust mote-
laden sunbeams as they crisscrossed throughout the darkened
interior of the cabin, forming little spears of light to stab
through the cracks in the walls and gaps and holes in the
shake-shingled roof. Now the bright spears of light were gone,
replaced by the dim glow of early evening.

When the outlaws came to the ranch, they had caught them
totally by surprise, killing her mother and father, shooting
down Ev, even as he was shooting two of them. When they
left the ranch, Lucy was their prisoner. There had been seven
then, but three of the men broke away not too long after they
left. Then another one of them, a Mexican, stayed back in
the little Mexican town they had come through. After leaving the little Mexican town, they rode hard, not even stopping
to eat, until they reached this shack, which Potter had evi-
dently known about. Now Potter was somewhat agitated that
none of the men who had ridden off had returned.

"Maybe the Coulters got 'em," one of the remaining men
suggested.

"They couldn't have killed all four of them," Potter replied.
"Hell, they didn't even know about the Mex. You want to

know what I think? I think the bastards ran out on us."

"They wouldn't run out on us, Potter. Hell, I know Mayhan wouldn't," Rawlings said. "I'm tellin' you, somethin' must've happened. Whyn't you let me and Cain and Smitty go back and wait on them? We'll pick us out some place and kill the sons of bitches from ambush."

"All right, Rawlings you three go ahead," Potter agreed. "I'll wait for you here. But as soon as the bastards are dead you come back here and tell me, you hear? You come back here and tell me."

"We'll come back," Rawlings promised.

That had been over two hours ago and they weren't back yet. As a result, Potter was pacing back and forth in the little cabin, going over to the window every couple of minutes to look outside.

"They aren't coming back," Lucy said.

"You," Potter said, turning away from the window and pointing at her, "just keep your mouth shut."

"I was just telling you what you already know," she said.

"I mean it," Potter said again. "Just keep your mouth shut or I'll gag you."

Lucy shut up, but she continued to watch Potter's every move, riveting him with her eyes. He broke out in a heavy sweat and kept wiping his face and the top of his head.

"Quiet!" he said a moment later, though she hadn't made a sound. "I hear someone." He drew his pistol and stood at the window, staring through it. Suddenly he turned around with a big grin on his face. "It's Rawlings," he said. "He's back. I guess you know what that means. The Coulters are dead." He walked over and looked down at the cot. "Not much point in keepin' you around any longer now, is there?" he asked.

Lucy heard the horse stop out front, then the door opened and Rawlings came bounding in.

"They killed Cain and Smitty," he said.

"What? I thought you were going to shoot them from ambush."

"Hell, we did," Rawlings said. "Or at least, we tried to. I

hit the big one, I knocked him down off his horse. Then Cain I don't know, he just went sort of crazy. Maybe it was because he thought I was goin' to get the credit or somethin'. Anyway, he just run out toward the big one, shooting wild, without even stopping to think that there was two of 'em. The other one come out of a draw then and shot Cain dead. Then that damn fool Smitty raised up and got himself shot dead too.''

"But you said you got the big one, right? You said you knocked him off his horse."

"Yeah, I did."

"Well?"

"Well, what?"

"Did you kill him, man? Did you kill him?"

"No, I don't think so. I think I just winged him or some-thin'."

"You don't think so," Potter said with a scornful snort.

"I know so. I didn't kill him," Rawlings said.

"All right. All right, then we'll just wait here for both of them."

"To hell with that. *You* wait for them," Rawlings said. "I ain't stayin' aroun' here. I've had enough. There ain't no way I'm goin' to go up against them Coulters again."

"You ain't runnin' out on me!" Potter said.

"You think not? You watch me. And if you got any sense, you'll run too. Come on, leave the girl an' let's go."

"We're staying," Potter insisted.

"I'm not staying," Rawlings said. "I wouldn't even stopped by here 'ceptin' to warn you." Rawlings started for the door but before he reached it, there was a gunshot, then a billow of smoke filled the cabin. Rawlings spun around with a surprised look on his face. He saw Potter standing there, holding the smoking gun in his hand. Rawlings put his hand around to his back, trying to find the bullet hole, but he couldn't reach it. "You son of a bitch, you shot me!" he said.

Rawlings pitched forward onto his face. He tried to get back up, raised up to his hands and knees, then went down again. This time he lay still and after a couple of gasping breaths, he was dead.

"I told you," Potter said under his breath. "You wasn't leavin'."

The night air felt refreshingly cool after the long, hot day. Win dismounted and stared at the cabin, some one hundred yards away.

"You think that's them?" Win asked.

"This is where the trail leads," Joe replied.

"I'm going to go up and take a look. You hang on to the horses."

"Why don't we hobble the horses and I'll go with you?" Joe suggested.

"No, you stay here," Win insisted. "No offense, Little Brother, but you aren't all that good at sneaking around."

"All right," Joe agreed. "But if you need me, I'll be here."

Win nodded at his brother, then slipped through the shadows until he was on the outside of the cabin. He edged along the wall until he could look through a gap between the boards. Incredibly, there was a candle burning inside, thus allowing him to see what was going on.

Win saw Lucy staked out on the bunk, and two men in the front of the cabin, looking out through the two front windows. Potter was very animated, moving back and forth nervously, while the other man was absolutely still. There was something strange about the second person, but Win didn't know what it was.

The problem, as Win saw it, was that there was only one way into the cabin, and that was through the front door. And Potter had the front door so well covered that there was no way he could get in without affording the outlaw a clear line of fire.

The cabin was old and had probably been abandoned for a long time. That explained all the gaps in the wall, the collapsed porch, and the caved-in roof.

There were no windows at the back of the cabin, so Win went around behind, found the exposed beam of a rafter and used it to pull himself up onto the roof. Lying on his stomach he moved across the top of the cabin, slowly, quietly, testing the shingles until he could find several that were loose and rotten. He pulled one aside, then looked through. Potter was still pacing around nervously, but the other man had not moved since the first time Win saw him.

"Where is he?" Win heard Potter ask. "Why don't he come?"

"He's waiting for you to make a mistake," Lucy said.

"Shut up!" Potter replied, whirling around toward her. He pointed his gun at her. "The only thing keepin' you alive now is I might need you. But if you don't keep that mouth of yours shut, I'll shoot you whether I need you or not."

Win realized that Potter was getting very nervous, and the more nervous he got, the more dangerous it would be for Lucy. He had to do something and he had to do it soon.

Win studied the roof for a moment, then saw that there was one area which was covered by four or five rotten shingles. He could break them off easily, but if he did, Potter would surely hear him the moment he started.

Then he got an idea. He wouldn't break them off one at a time, he would break them off all at once. But the only way he could do that would be to jump right through them. And that meant a drop of eight to ten feet to the floor below.

Win stood up quietly, took a deep breath, then leaped right into the middle of the rotten shingles, then crashed through.

Lucy was as shocked as Potter when she saw Win suddenly burst through the roof and fall to the floor. She let out a little scream of surprise.

"What the hell!" Potter shouted, swinging around from the window to blaze away at the intruder. A long finger of flame spit from the end of his gun and the heavy slug tore into the floor where Win landed. It would have hit Win, had Win not rolled to his left the moment he fell. Win fired as he rolled, and Potter went down, clawing at a hole next to his heart. Win rolled again and turned his gun toward the second man, who still hadn't turned around.

"He's dead!" Lucy shouted.

Win, seeing that the second man was, indeed, dead, lowered his gun.

"Potter shot him when he thought he was going to run

away," Lucy went on. "He stuck him up in the window to fool you into thinking there were two of them in here."

Win chuckled. "It worked," he said. "I was fooled." He put his gun away then, and went over to the cot to untie the ropes that held Lucy bound. "Are you all right?"

"Yes," Lucy said. As soon as she was untied, she ringed Win's neck with her arms and hugged him hard. "Thank you," she said. "I knew you would come."

"It's all over now," Win said, gently. "Joe's outside. We'll take you back home."

"Home?" Lucy said. Tears came to her eyes. "What's there to go home to? Ma and Pa are both dead. So's Ev. And the ranch is burned."

"The buildings are burned," Win said. "But the land is still there. So are the cattle." He smiled. "And so is Ev."

"What?" Lucy gasped. "But I saw him . . ."

"You saw Ev shot," Win interrupted. "But he didn't die and he's not going to."

"Thank God," Lucy said, crying with relief.

"Have you had anything to eat?"

"No, not since I was captured."

"Why don't I get Joe in here to fix us something to eat? Then we'll rest here tonight and leave at first light."

Chapter 20

WHEN JARRED SNELL CAME ACROSS CAIN AND SMITTY'S bodies, he chuckled.

"Oh, you Coulter boys are good all right," he said to himself. "You're damn good. Maybe even the best around . . . next to me." He stood up and walked over to his horse and patted the polished stock of the Whitworth. "By this time tomorrow, I'll have both of you belly-down across your horses."

Snell had already heard the story, how Potter had burned out the Truelove Ranch, killed the girl's parents, and stolen the girl. Win and Joe Coulter had gone after her.

There were some back in Paso del Muerte who figured the Coulters had bitten off more than they could chew. Potter had at least half a dozen outlaws he could call upon. There were only two of the Coulters.

Snell hadn't believed for one moment that the Coulters were in over their heads. Then, as he began following the bloody trail they were leaving behind, he knew the Coulters would find the girl. And once they found her, they would have to bring her back to Paso del Muerte. All Snell would have to do is wait for them.

Some might wonder why Snell was so doggedly determined to bring the Coulters in. After all, even after he killed them, he would have to get an affidavit signed by an officer of the court, verifying that they were dead, then he would have to present that affidavit to a court official in the state of Kansas.

Kansas might be the only place where a reward was still in effect, but the state of Kansas wasn't the only one who wanted them dead. The thing that had brought Snell here in the first place was a letter of employment. The terms of employment were very simple. All he had to do was kill Win and Joe Coulter.

Snell pulled out a piece of jerky and began chewing. He washed it down with a swallow of water, then hobbled his horse and threw out his blankets. May as well get some sleep, he thought. The Coulters wouldn't be through there before tomorrow.

A hot dry wind moved through the canyon, pushing before it a billowing puff of red dust. The cloud of dust lifted high and spread out wide and made it look as if there were blood on the sun.

Four horses came into the canyon. Win, Joe, and Lucy were the three riders. Potter's cold, lifeless body was belly-down on the fourth horse.

It was mid-morning and they had been riding since first light. Now, with Potter and most of his henchmen dead, there didn't seem much need to keep on the razor's edge of alertness. That was good, because Joe was running a little fever from his shoulder wound and Win kept looking around at him every so often.

Joe chuckled. "You think I can't stay in the saddle, Big Brother?"

"I don't know," Win answered. "I'm thinking about tying you on your horse."

"Long as it's not belly-down like ole' Potter here," Joe replied.

Win wondered how his brother could keep going. He wasn't wounded, but even he could feel the weariness creeping in, and as he sat in the saddle and let the sun warm his back, his eyelids began to grow heavy and he let his guard down.

The heavy slug whizzed by him, less than an inch in front of his nose. It hit a rock then let out a banshee whine as it flew away. Win's hair stood on end and his stomach rose to his throat as he was instantly awake. The deep boom of a distant rifle shot reached his ears.

"It's Snell!" Win shouted.

"What?"

"Come on!" Win called, slapping his legs against the side of his horse and urging him off the trail. He jerked the reins on Potter's horse so that it, Joe and Lucy followed him.

There was a second shot and this time the bullet hit one of the spans of a pear cactus. The cactus exploded into little pieces.

"Get under there!" Win shouted, pointing to a rock overhang. They rode behind the cover just as a third shot was fired. Win swung down from his horse, reached up and literally pulled Lucy down. He shoved her head down behind a rock and he and Joe got down with her. They were safe there. Snell would have to come up on them to get a shot, and that would bring him into Win's range.

"Who'd you say that was?" Joe asked.

"Jarred Snell. You know . . . the bounty hunter who killed Fenton? I think he's also the one who killed my horse."

"If he's a bounty hunter, why the hell is he after us? We aren't wanted in any state except Kansas."

"May not be a state," Win explained.

"What do you mean?"

"I have a feeling some individual has put a reward on us."

"Damn!" Snell said as he reloaded his rifle. He'd seen where the Coulters and the girl ran and he knew he couldn't get a shot at them from there.

Snell stood up and stretched, took a few steps back from where he had been sitting, and dipped his hand down into the stream, then raised it to his mouth to take a drink. He laughed.

"How much water you folks got in your canteen?" he asked under his breath. "How long can you wait?"

Snell walked back over to his perch on the high rock and waited. The Coulters and the girl would have to come out some time.

● ● ●

It was late in the afternoon when Snell saw them. At first he wasn't sure it was them, there was only a slight movement way down below. Then, as he looked closely, he saw what was going on.

Two riders were leaning low over the neck of their horses, moving slowly though a twisting ravine, behind an outcropping of rocks and a screen of mesquite. Snell hadn't noticed that possible escape route when he set up his ambush. They almost made it through, would have, perhaps, had it not been that Snell caught a flash of red, the girl's dress, out of the corner of his eye.

"Well now," Snell said. "Aren't you the clever ones? You've found a little ravine that leads out of there, haven't you?"

Snell looked around quickly, then saw another rock, perhaps a hundred yards away and fifty feet higher. It would make the shot more difficult, but he was sure that from that vantage point, he would be able to see them when they emerged at the far end of the ravine. And if he could see them, he could kill them.

Snell hurried to the new position. He had time, not only because the ravine twisted and turned for quite a ways until it ran out, but also because the two riders were moving very slowly so as not to attract his attention. As a result, he was in position, lying on his stomach, with the scope to his eye, when the two horses emerged.

"How come there is only one of you and the girl?" he asked. "Where's the other one?"

He looked around, very carefully, to make certain that the second brother wasn't sneaking up on him. When he was sure that he wasn't, he got back in position and waited for the riders to appear. He may have hit the other brother. At any rate, he would take care of him later. A bird in hand was better than two birds in the bush.

The moment the two riders came out of the ravine, the horses broke into a gallop.

"Ha!" Snell said. "Do you think you are clear?"

Snell aimed at the target, held it in his scope for a moment, then squeezed the trigger slowly. Even as he was rocked back by the recoil of the exploding cartridge he could see a puff of dust fly away from the back of Coulter's shirt. Coulter fell from his horse.

The girl's horse continued on for a few feet, then stopped and came back. Snell opened the breech and slipped in another shell. He thought about killing the girl too, then decided against it. He wasn't getting paid to kill her. He laughed, then hurried back to his horse, slipped the Whitworth back into the saddle sheath, and started the long ride down to claim his prize.

Money in the bank as soon as he delivered the body to Paso del Muerte, then another $1,500 as soon as he managed to get verification of the killing to the proper authorities in Kansas.

But it wasn't just the money. No, sir. It was the satisfaction.

He recalled that time during the war, when one of the Coulters was giving aid and comfort to the enemy. Considering that treasonous, he'd tried to stop him, but the other one had come up behind him and hit him on the head.

Yes, sir, he had waited a long, long time for this.

As Snell drew closer, he saw that the red dress was kneeling beside the body. What was the girl doing there? Why hadn't she ridden on while she had the chance? Maybe he should go ahead and kill her. He knew that the man who was paying him for Win Coulter also wanted the girl dead. He was the one who set up the raid on the girl's ranch in the first place. Maybe there would be a bonus for him if he brought in not only Coulter's body, but the girl's as well. He had never killed a woman before, but when he stopped to think about it, he didn't suppose it mattered all that much. Killing was killing.

Snell pulled his shotgun from the other saddle sheath, opened it to check the load, then snapped it shut. As he drew closer still, he urged the horse into a trot and raised the gun.

Suddenly the figure in red stood up and turned around to face Snell.

"What?" Snell gasped.

It wasn't the girl! It was Win Coulter, wearing the girl's dress! Almost as soon as he realized that, he saw, also, that Coulter had a gun in his hand.

• • •

Win fired and saw a puff of dust leap from Snell's shirt. Snell pitched back out of the saddle as the shotgun flew out of his hand. His foot hung up in the stirrup and his horse bolted, dragging him across the hard, rocky ground for several feet before the foot came undone. Win hurried over to look down at him. When he got there he saw that Snell was still alive, though only barely.

"You look awful funny in that dress," Snell said. His voice was strained.

"Yeah," Win said. "I wouldn't want to ride into town like this."

"Pretty smart," Snell admitted. "Who . . . who the hell did I kill?"

"Nobody," Win said. "He was already dead. That was Potter, wearing my clothes and my hat."

"I'll be a son of a bitch."

"Who you working for, Snell? Surely you didn't come this far on a Kansas warrant?"

"Ain't you figured that out yet, Coulter? We been feedin' at the same trough." Snell began to laugh. "The same trough," he said. "That's good. That's real good." He laughed again, but the laughing changed to a spasmadic coughing, then he gasped once, and the breathing ended with one final death rattle.

"Is he dead?"

When Win looked up, he saw Joe and Lucy. Lucy was wearing only a petticoat and chemise, and she kept her arms across her breast, preserving some modesty, if not her dignity.

"Yeah," Win said. "He's dead. Now, what do you say we get back into our right clothes?"

"Oh, I don't know, Win . . . I think you look just real nice," Joe teased.

As they were changing clothes, Win thought about what Snell said about them feeding at the same trough. Then he thought of something else that had been bothering him, though it had been at the very back of his mind until now.

"Lucy. On the morning Potter raided your ranch, why was your father home?"

"What do you mean, why was he home?"

"I thought he had to run over to Sweetwater that day."

"No."

"Are you sure?"

"Yes, of course I'm sure," Lucy said. "We were all waiting on the other ranchers to come over and help us put on a new roof that day. She laughed. "Anyway, Pa hated Sweetwater. He claimed the feed store over there cheated him. He'd go out of his way to avoid the place."

When the little party rode into Paso del Muerte the next day, they attracted quite a bit of attention. A young boy saw them first and he went running back into town to shout the news. Others came out then and the crowd of citizens formed a parade as they ran along the street alongside the four horses.

"They brought the girl back safe," someone said.

"Who's that belly-down on the horse?" another asked.

"Why, that there's Potter."

"They done it! By God, they cleaned 'em all out!"

Ev met them about halfway through town, and though one arm was in a sling and he was getting along on crutches, he hobbled out into the middle of the street to greet Lucy. She slid down from her horse and ran to him.

"Win, Joe, thanks," Ev said.

Win smiled at the young cowboy, then he saw his brother weaving back and forth in his saddle.

"Ev, Lucy, do me a favor, will you? Get Joe to the doctor."

"No, I'm all right," Joe said. "A couple night's rest and I'll be fine."

"Couple nights more without getting that tended to, and you might be dead," one of the townspeople said, and he and another helped Joe down from his horse.

"Where you goin', Win?"

"I've got some business to tend to," Win answered.

Win continued on through town until he reached the Cattlemen's Association Building. From the horses and buggies gathered out front, he saw that a meeting was in session. That was good, that was just what he wanted.

Win pulled Potter's body off the pack horse, threw it across his shoulder, then packed it into the building.

"Coulter! You're back!" Claymore said. He had been sitting at the head of the table and he stood up as Win entered the room.

"I've got a package for you," Win said, dumping Potter's body onto the table. Several of the ranchers recoiled in horror.

"That's a rather gruesome package to deliver in here, isn't it?" Claymore scolded. "Couldn't you have just left him on the street?"

"I suppose I could have," Win said. "But I thought you might want to see him. You know, this means you'll have to get someone else now."

"Yes, I know, your work is all done," Claymore said. "But we won't need anyone else now."

"That's not what I'm talking about. I mean you, Doc Claymore, are going to have to get someone else to do your dirty work, now that your man, Potter, is dead."

"My man?"

"Look here, Coulter, what the Sam Hill are you talking about?" Baker asked.

"Yeah, that's what I'd like to know," demanded Claymore.

"What I'm talking about is the fact that Potter worked for Doc Claymore," Win said.

"What?" the others asked.

"How dare you say such a thing?" Claymore blustered. "Why, this is preposterous."

"Is it? Why did you hire Snell to kill my brother and me?"

"What makes you think I did?"

Win tossed a letter onto the table. "I took this off his body," Win said. "After he tried to kill me."

"What is that?" Vogel asked, as Baker picked it up.

Baker read the letter, then looked over at Claymore. "It's a letter," he said, "offering $2,500 to Snell for each of the Coulters."

"Is that true, Doc?" Masters asked.

"Well, what if it is? The Coulters are wanted men. They rode with Quantrill for chrissake. Kansas has a reward out for him. I was just supplementing the reward, that's all. There's nothing illegal about that."

"But why would you want to do that? Coulter was cleaning out the rustlers for us."

"I haven't made any secret of the fact that I've been against all the killing," Claymore said. "I was just trying to stop it the only way I knew how, that's all." He looked at Win. "Now, if you think you can reason from that, that I was the head of this rustling operation, then I'd like to know how."

"Yeah, Coulter, that's a pretty far reach," Baker said. "How do you come up with such a conclusion?"

"I'll leave it up to you to figure out who has gained every time one of the other ranchers is forced out," Win said. "And I'll leave it up to you to find the missing cows somewhere on Claymore's land. But I do have one question for Claymore. Do you remember the meeting the other morning? The day Truelove's ranch was burned out? Who called the meeting?"

"Doc Claymore," Vogel said.

"I'm the President. It's my right to call the meetings," Claymore said.

"Yes, and you told the others that Truelove wouldn't be coming to the meeting because he was going to Sweetwater."

"That's what he told me."

"You're lying. You never told him about the meeting. And the only reason you called one was to make sure none of these men were out at Truelove's ranch when Potter and his bunch made their raid."

"You're crazy."

Win looked over at Baker and Vogel. "Think about it, men. Do you remember what you were supposed to do that morning?"

"The roof!" Vogel said. "We were going to help Truelove put on a new roof."

"Yeah," Baker said. "Why would he go to Sweetwater if . . ."

"Look out! Claymore's pulled a gun!" one of the men shouted.

Win spun around toward Claymore. He had been expecting this, had hoped for it in fact, and when he saw the gun in Claymore's hand he pulled his own, drawing and firing in the same, fluid, motion, doing it so quickly that the noise of his shot covered Claymore's so that they sounded as one, even though Claymore had fired a split second sooner.

Claymore's bullet whizzed by harmlessly, burying itself in the wall behind Win. Win's bullet caught Claymore right between the eyes. The president of the Paso del Muerte Cattlemen's Association fell back with his arms flopping down to either side, and his head lolled back against the back of the chair. Both eyes were open but there was a third opening, a small, black hole, right at the bridge of his nose. Actually, only a small amount of blood trickled from the hole, though the chair-back cushion was already stained red with the blood that had gushed out from the exit wound.

The ranchers looked at Claymore's body in shock. It had all happened so fast that, for a moment, they could almost believe that it hadn't happened at all, that Claymore had merely sat back down in his seat. But the drifting cloud of acrid smoke said otherwise.

"Is he dead?" Baker asked.

"As a doornail," someone answered.

Baker looked back toward Win, who had now put his gun away and was looking at Claymore with eyes that were totally devoid of expression.

"Mr. Coulter, I reckon we owe you some apologies," Baker said.

"No, Baker," Win said. "What you owe me is some money."

JAKE LOGAN
TODAY'S HOTTEST ACTION WESTERN!